THE GRAVEL ROAD

Rise and Fall
of a Music Icon

A Novel by
RON BRUNK

ISBN 978-0-989737-23-4 (eBook)
ISBN 978-0-9897372-4-1 (pbk)

Library of Congress Control Number 2013917409

Alexia Publishing
PO Box 120942
Nashville, TN 37212

www.AlexiaPublishing.com

www.RonBrunk.com

ronbrunk@yahoo.com

For the true artists
Who see no boxes
And refuse to circle the wagons.

The Gravel Road

Part One

1

After days of hurricane rains, the Great Lawn in Central Park had become muddy pandemonium, and the throngs of people churned and roiled as one, like a great beast in the throes of passion, as Gravel Gold prepared to make his grand entrance onto the stage. The excitement and anticipation in the audience was off the chart with energy so powerful, so palpable that I could actually *see* it as it rolled over the crowd and struck me in the chest.

Gravel Gold did not come to the stage by skydiving onto it, swinging from a rope like Tarzan, being lifted up on a sunken platform, or by riding a zebra through the crowd. He'd done all those things, and more, before. Instead, he surprised us all by appearing out of an eight-foot-tall sky box that was suspended on scaffolding fifty feet above the stage. No one in the band knew exactly how or when he got up there, but the box suddenly opened and there he was. Gravel stepped out onto the edge of the sky box and stood silently, high above us. The crowd of 1.2 million people exploded with a deafening roar at the sight of him, but Gravel Gold remained motionless, unmoved and unmoving. One minute passed…two minutes went by. The roar diminished and eventually turned as quiet as 1.2 million puzzled humans could possibly be, watching and waiting for what the crazy man might do.

Guitar in hand, I stood on the stage and stared up, studying him closely. In addition to his usual rhinestone-studded, black apparel, Gravel was also wearing thick, black gloves, and a small apparatus similar to the lower half of a gas mask strapped around his jaws. *What in the world is that, and what's he up to this time?* I wondered.

Gravel's entrances usually took us completely by surprise because he rarely told anyone – not even me, his closest confidant – about them in advance. As in the military, information was distributed strictly on a 'need to know' basis. Gravel preferred the spontaneity, creativity, and unparalleled danger that came from living on the edge. He was willing to risk everything for the glory of the moment. The only members of the staff who knew about his stunts beforehand were those who helped him prepare and conduct them. They were, of course, sworn to secrecy, no matter how dangerous the exploit. "Breathe a word of it, and you're gone, and you'll never work in this business again," he'd tell them.

Suddenly, Gravel raised his gloved hands into the air, and great jets of flame shot from the mask on his face, setting both hands ablaze. He stood there holding huge balls of fire above his head as the crowd became wild and frenzied. Then, like Zeus casting lightning bolts, Gravel flung fireballs, one after another, high into the air where they burned madly into the night sky before dissipating.

An automated ramp descended from the box to the stage at a forty-five degree angle; and Gravel raced down it, grabbed his guitar, and began playing viciously like some misbegotten bastard child of Jimi Hendrix and Chet Atkins, as if the scattered seed of Robert Johnson and Kurt Cobain had somehow come to rest in his soul and to roost in his loins. He commanded his legions, absorbed the energies of 1.2 million screaming humans, and pounded out raging riffs like angry chunks of beef in a boiling stew of narcissism and unabated musical ambition.

Blister slowly laid down a tribal beat behind Gravel, and the rest of us followed his lead. Though some people still thought of Gravel Gold as a country music star, as he originally had been, there was nothing 'country' about what we were doing. It was pure rock madness and excruciating beauty. We built and climbed a ladder of sound, soaring toward a collapse and plunging into a crescendo.

Gravel breathed fire onto his hands again, setting both them and the guitar ablaze. Still, he played on, lost in the power and glory of the moment, until his pyrotechnic gloves began to disintegrate and the heat became unbearable. He smashed the flaming, melting guitar on the stage before him, and cast more fireballs at it as the crowd chanted to their idol: *Gravel Gold. Gravel Gold. Gravel Gold. Gravel Gold.*

The music icon stood center stage with arms spread wide and absorbed the adulation for several minutes. Then he pulled off the flame-throwing mask, threw it into the crowd, picked up an acoustic guitar and played softly, completely shifting gears and altering the atmosphere. The crowd went deathly still as he sang:

> *I've run aground on gravel bars,*
> *Where the river was dark and muddy,*
> *Burned my lips on shooting stars*
> *That left me blind and bloody,*
>
> *I'm riding the crest of a fearsome wave,*
> *Wounded and weary, battered but brave,*
> *With one foot in my future,*
> *And the other one in my grave.*

2

The Presidential Suite was packed that night after the show, and the party raged until the sun kissed Manhattan with morning lips. Gravel Gold swaggered erratically from room to room, working the crowd, chain-smoking Camel cigarettes, and taking great gulps from a bottle of Jim Beam. And those of us in Gravel's inner circle knew full well that he had much more than nicotine and whiskey in his system.

When the cameras were rolling or when he was in a crowd, Gravel could be a likeable, charming Louisiana boy, albeit rough-edged, always ready with an amusing anecdote or entertaining expression. He was like a cross between a Cajun Will Rogers and a folksy Darth Vader, and the media considered him the indisputable king of the sound-bite. Gravel was a tough son of a bitch, a blistering guitar player, and women swooned when he tipped his black hat and burned his dark eyes into their souls.

Most people might have relished the opportunity to be a part of Gravel Gold's entourage and endless party, but I'd never really craved the light, neither lime nor spot. While the rest of Gravel's band, crew and hangers-on milled about the suite, eating from the impressive spread of food and mingling with the long line of A-List visitors, I surveyed the scene silently from a shadowy corner, and observed the carnival-like atmosphere and crush of circus freaks that followed Gravel wherever he went. *My God, how in the world did I end up here? I never wanted this; I just wanted to write songs.*

"Benji! Where's Benji?" Gravel suddenly shouted. Benji was Benjamin Wallows, Gravel's personal assistant, a slight man with sandy hair who wore wire-rimmed glasses, khakis and a yellow sweater vest. Listening intently to his headset, working his computer or iPad, or fumbling nervously through papers on a clipboard, he always looked completely out of place in the rock star environment. But he was brilliant, highly efficient, and Gravel trusted him fully and depended on him.

"Yes, Mr. Gold, here I am," Benji said, working his way through the crowd.

Gravel put a big arm around his assistant and pulled him close. "Benji, I got an idea. Go downstairs, pick out a bunch of them damn press vultures, and tell security to let 'em up here. I got some things to say."

Samuel Peters, Vice President of Gravel's record label, GMI, was standing nearby and overheard Gravel's suggestion. Samuel had helped organize last night's show, Gravel Gold's historic Concert in Central Park. He'd been on site for months helping coordinate the massive event with the Police, the Mayor's Office, and the New York City Parks and Recreation Department. So far, the entire event had gone reasonably well – a rarity for a Gravel Gold show – and Samuel hoped to keep it that way. He didn't want to see it all crumble at the after party or on the following morning.

"Uh, Gravel," Samuel Peters said. "I don't know if that's a very good idea."

"That's because you don't know shit," Gravel said, patting him lightly on the cheek with an open palm. "Relax, Sammy, and trust me."

Oh, yeah, that'll work, I thought.

Amused, I watched Sammy and some of the other label representatives tug nervously at their ties and shirt

11

collars. Everyone was aware of Gravel Gold's reputation for putting his foot in his mouth, or occasionally up someone's ass.

While we waited, Gravel started on a fresh fifth of Jim Beam, wiped his mouth with the back of his hand and slung an arm around my shoulders. "Trotter," he said, his bourbon breath stinging my eyes, "Watch and learn, my boy, watch and learn."

In a few minutes, a large group of reporters rushed into the room, battling for position, shouting out questions, filming, and snapping pictures. Gravel stepped into their midst, head and shoulders above them all. He was a big man, the size of a defensive lineman in professional football, but with chiseled features and sculpted muscles. All of Gravel's attire was studded with thousands of glimmering rhinestones and his trademark "GG" initials. Clad fully in black, including cowboy boots and hat, he made an outrageous yet impressive figure. He was retro-country, street-smart tough guy, and rock star groove all at the same time; and, depending on his mood, he could be delightful, self-deprecating, or extremely dangerous.

"Howdy, folks," he spoke into the mass of cameras and microphones with a blend of authority and down-home charm. "I know ya'll got plenty to keep ya busy here in the Big Apple, so I sure do appreciate how many of ya'll came out to our show last night. Ya'll know me…I'm just an average Joe from down in the Cajun swamps, and me and my good buddies came here to the greatest city on earth to make a little music and spread some joy. We are truly touched with the outpouring of love we felt from everyone."

My God, gag me with a spoon. What a load of crap.

While he had their undivided attention, Gravel paused and chugged half a bottle of bourbon. No one could drink like Gravel - not even me, and I considered myself an expert guzzler. Then Gravel lit an unfiltered Camel, took a long draw, and casually blew clouds of smoke into their faces. Some of them coughed and gagged, and a few grumbled objections about second-hand smoke. Because I knew Gravel so well, I knew exactly what he was thinking: *Pussies.*

"I wanna read you folks somethin'," Gravel said, turning deathly serious. "No one knows about this, but it's somethin' I been carryin' around with me for years. Ain't told a soul about it till this very moment. Now you guys are the lucky ones to get the scoop."

Gravel pulled a tattered newspaper clipping from his pocket and held it with trembling hands. Then he motioned conspiratorially for the reporters to lean in closer as if he was about to share the secrets of the universe with them. You could have heard a guitar pick drop.

Gravel read from the paper, his gravelly Cajun voice cracking with emotion, "On Aug. 7, 1997, Garth Brooks drew the largest crowd ever to attend a concert in New York's Central Park - 750,000. 'Garth Live From Central Park,' airing on HBO, was the highest rated original program on HBO in 1997, as well as the most-watched special on cable television in 1997, drawing 14.6 million television viewers."

He paused for a long while for dramatic effect, and wiped at his eyes with the back of his hand, as though fighting back tears.

"Last night my lifelong dream was fulfilled – I broke Garth's record that had stood all these years. And it's thanks to you good people."

A reporter from *Time* shouted, "Mr. Gold, some estimates put the attendance for that Garth Brooks show as high as 980,000. How can you be so sure you beat his number?"

"Don't the number 1.2 million mean anything to you?" Gravel snarled with a quick change of emotional gears. "I don't know how you figure it where you come from, but where I come from, 1.2 million beats the hell out of 980,000."

Another reporter shouted, "How can you make a claim like that? Our estimates put last night's attendance at 950,000."

"Your estimates!?" Gravel shouted. "You think anybody gives a damn about *your* estimates?" Then he spun around suddenly, threw his whiskey bottle across the room, and smashed it against the wall, startling everyone…everyone but me. I calmly watched the heavy Jim Beam bottle literally explode upon impact. Millions of miniscule glass slivers hung like a mist in the air, shimmering in the morning sunlight that had broken through the clouds and was streaming through the windows.

Sure is pretty.

Gravel Gold turned back toward the reporters and flashed his familiar, mischievous grin. "Thought I saw a damn mosquito over there," he said, motioning toward the wall. "Lord knows we hate mosquitoes down in the swamp."

"Gravel, if you don't mind, I'd like to address the attendance issue," Samuel Peters, the label representative said. "Ladies and gentlemen of the media, let me assure you on behalf of GMI Records that we calculated attendance with state-of-the-art equipment using a fully integrated digital system of computers, sensors, monitors, satellite imagery, and GPS technologies. We also had a trained team of people on the ground and in the air via helicopters and other small aircraft. By gathering and assessing data in this manner, we were able to provide the ultimate in security while also compiling the first truly accurate attendance figures ever for a free event such as this."

"Truly an incredibly ambitious and brilliant undertaking, Mr. Gold," a loud voice announced from the back of the room. It was Jimmy Bolen, President of GMI International, Gravel Gold's record label, and the man who had worked tirelessly for a year to help arrange for Gravel's concert in Central Park to be broadcast live around the world.

Bolen was attired in an exquisite, grey Givenchy two-button suit with chalk stripes and double vents. A lavender tie traced his sternum and Berluti Classics graced his feet. He wore a Rolex Deepsea Classic wristwatch and a diamond ring that had more carats than my grandmother's garden. His dark hair was pushed up and back in early James Dean style, and his chin jutted forward in the manner of a man who was accustomed to getting his way.

Seizing the perfect photo-op moment, Bolen grabbed Gravel's hand and shook it vigorously. "Congratulations, Gravel," he said, smiling big, too big for my liking, like a happy serpent. "The biggest star in the world gave humanity the biggest show in the world. We made history yesterday, my friend...*history.*"

"Yeah, *we* made history," Gravel replied sarcastically. "I was the one out there on stage for three hours last night, bustin' my ass, playin' my guitar, singin' the songs that I wrote while you were sittin' on your ass makin' money off my sweat and talent. I didn't hear anybody chanting *your* name. I didn't see anybody worshipping you."

Perfect. He just humiliated the president of one of the largest record labels in the world in front of a room full of reporters and cameras. Gravel had no qualms about biting the hand that fed him or burning bridges he hadn't even crossed yet.

Jimmy Bolen's face flushed for only a moment before the calculated smile returned. "There's no denying, ladies and gentlemen, that Mr. Gravel Gold does indeed put on a show like no other, and he's certainly the hardest working son of a bitch in the industry. That's why we're so proud to have him on GMI."

"You got that right, Jimmy. I gave 'em a show they'll never forget," Gravel said, slinging a big arm around Bolen's shoulders, and hugging me close. Gravel did that often. It was his way of disarming you, making you feel like the two of you were best buddies from way back, even if he'd just punched you in the face.

3

"Alright, everybody out!" Gravel shouted as he roved through the rooms, fresh whiskey bottle in hand, rousing guests who were in a drunken stupor, using the pointy tip of his black cowboy boot to poke those who lay passed out on the floor. "Party's over. Thanks for comin'. Now get the hell out."

Soon Gravel, Benji, Addie and I were alone in what was left of the beautiful penthouse, which looked as though someone had detonated a nuclear garbage bomb in the living room.

"Shouldn't you get some sleep, Mr. Gold?" Benji asked cautiously, checking his PDA. "You have a one o'clock photo-op with the mayor and other city officials, and a four o'clock with Mr. Bolen and the label reps. After that, dinner at seven with Madonna and--"

"Change of plan, Benji, boy," Gravel interrupted.

"But what about--"

"You go in my place, Benji. Give 'em my regrets."

"But sir, I can't…what do I tell them?"

"Tell 'em I got the swine flu or malaria or somethin'. No, wait, tell 'em I was overwhelmed by the events of last night – yeah, that's it. And that I was emotionally drained by the entire glorious experience and the outpouring of love from my fans. You know, all that typical BS. Lay it on thick."

Benjamin Wallows looked like a man at the end of his rope. He stood frozen in the center of the room, arms clutching papers, PDA, and laptop to his chest. "I have to go to dinner…with Madonna?" His voice trembled. I couldn't tell for sure if it was from excitement or fear.

Gravel was fond of his faithful assistant, so he leaned in close and took a different tack. "Now, Benji, I know you put up with more of my crap than anybody, maybe even more than my wife–"

Benjamin raised his hand in the air and said, "Excuse me, sir, but speaking of your wife…she has called three times from Italy."

"Yeah?" Gravel said slowly. "What's she want?"

"Apparently, she's dissatisfied with the Film Director. I think she's holed up in her dressing room in protest."

"That woman would punch a gift horse smack dab in the mouth," Gravel said. "I got her that big movie role and all she does is bitch and moan."

"Perhaps you should call her back," Benjamin suggested.

"Perhaps," Gravel grinned. "Perhaps someone should."

"You want me to call her," Benjamin stated flatly. "And explain to her that you are completely covered over with your obligations here in New York, and that you simply do not have even a minute to yourself, to do the things you would really like to do, like call her."

"You read my mind," Gravel said. "Benji, that's why I pay you the big bucks – 'because you're really good at what ya do and I know I can count on ya. How 'bout this…let's just say there'll be a bonus in your paycheck this month, an extra fifty thousand. Will that help?"

Benjamin nodded slowly and a look of firm resolve came over him. "Yes, sir, I will handle things today. You can trust me."

"Good, good," Gravel said, slapping him on the back, and nearly knocking him over in the process. "Now, there's just one more little thing I need ya to do. Tell the media and fans downstairs that I'll be giving a press conference in the hotel's Grand Ballroom in about an hour. Tell 'em I'll answer every question they have, sign autographs, pose for pictures, all that crap. Make it sound real good."

Benjamin studied Gravel and said very slowly, "There's not really going to be a press conference, is there?"

"You're sharp as a tack, Benji boy," Gravel said. "The press conference is just a diversion so that we can get the hell outta here."

"Sir, you know that Mr. Bolen won't be at all happy about this," Benjamin said.

"You just let me handle Bolen," Gravel said. "Now get on it…time's wastin'."

Benjamin rushed from the room as Gravel turned toward Addie, my girlfriend, and said, "Darlin', I got a little errand I want you to run. Need you to buy us a car."

Addie perked up a bit from where she'd been sprawled out, half asleep on a silk divan, an empty champagne glass hanging loosely in one hand, a roach clip in the other. "Uh, what? Do what?"

"Hold out your hand," he said to Addie. Gravel pulled a wad of bills from his pocket and counted out ten thousand dollars. "I want you to buy us a car."

"Buy a car? Is this enough money? What kind of car?"

"Just any crappy old used car…whatever you can get for ten grand. It's got to have plenty of leg room and lots of space…but it can't be nothin' fancy. You understand? We got to be inconspicuous to make our getaway."

"Getaway?" I asked, but Gravel ignored me.

19

Addie bit the inside of her cheek and studied the cash in her hands. "But where? How?" she stammered, trying to get her brain working.

"There's a used car lot two streets up. I think it's on 7th," Gravel said. "Flutter those pretty eyelashes, flash a little cash, and, believe me, some salesman will piss all over himself to sell you a car."

"I think I should go with her," I suggested.

"No, Trots, somebody's bound to recognize you. This has to be totally under the radar. I want to get outta New York without anybody knowin' about it or followin' us," Gravel said. "But I will have Booger" – he was one of the guards outside the door – "shadow her just to be safe."

Gravel turned back toward Addie, and said, "Darlin', when ya get the car, just bring it down the alley back of the building, by the loading docks. Park out of sight between the trailers and call us."

"Hey, if I can find something for, say, five thousand, can I keep the other five?" Addie asked with a grin, dimples dancing.

Gravel laughed loudly, lifted her up in his arms, and kissed her madly on the lips. It happened so quickly that I was taken completely by surprise. After a moment, Addie broke off the kiss and the embrace, but not nearly as quickly as I would've liked.

"Damn, you are one sweet little thing," Gravel said, putting her down. "Alright, let's get to packin'. And we're travelin' light, so only pack the necessities like weed, alcohol, a guitar, and your toothbrush."

When Gravel left the room, I finally found my voice. "What the hell was *that*?"

Addie, obviously flustered, said, "What? That? Oh, come on, Trotter, he was just fooling around." She put her arms around my neck and rubbed up against me. "You know how he is. I don't pay any attention when he acts like that."

20

I was silent and unmoving in the center of the room, just as Benji had been minutes before, suddenly feeling very uncertain.

"Hey, I've got to buy a car!" Addie shouted, breaking the spell. She put on dark glasses, wrapped herself in a long serape, and covered her head with a scarf. Striking a model's pose with her lips squished together in a kiss-like expression, she asked, "How do you like my disguise? Would you know me if you passed me on the street?"

"No, right about now, I don't think I would," I said.

4

It was a white Ford Bronco, and Addie sat behind the wheel, smiling proudly.

Gravel bent over in laughter on the loading dock when he saw the vehicle. "The OJ-Mobile! She bought the freakin' OJ-Mobile! Lord, if that don't beat everything I've ever seen."

"What? What is it?" Addie asked, genuinely puzzled, her voice rising an octave. "What's an OJ-Mobile?"

"Never mind, Addie," I chuckled. "It was a little before your time."

Still laughing, we hurriedly threw our guitars and bags in the back of the vehicle before anyone could spot us. Gravel said, "You drive, Trots, since you don't like to toke. Addie and me are gonna burn one and crack open a fresh bottle for breakfast."

They slipped into the back seat, I took the wheel, and we disappeared into the New York traffic. I sliced the Big Apple smoothly, weaving in and out of make-shift lanes with the grace and grit of an old-school, midtown cabbie. Later, rolling west on the Jersey Turnpike, Gravel mooned a toll booth worker.

Juvenile delinquent.

Gravel's cell phone rang. He handed it to me and instructed me to answer it on speaker. It was Samuel Peters with GMI and he wanted to speak with Gravel. He sounded upset.

"Uh, he's um, asleep. Totally exhausted from last night," I lied. "This is Trotter. Can I help?"

"Gravel called a press conference for the top of the hour, but he hasn't shown up. Where is he?"

I looked at Gravel and he smiled and shook his head NO.

"He's asleep…unavailable."

Suddenly, label President Jimmy Bolen got on the line. "I want Gravel on the damn phone, and I want him *now*."

Again, Gravel shook his head.

"I know he's listening to me. I'm on speaker, aren't I? Gravel, you son of a bitch, where the hell are you?"

Long silence.

"Listen, you can't keep doing this. You called a press conference and didn't show up. And now you have a meeting in less than an hour with the Mayor of New York City. This is totally unacceptable behavior. I swear to God if you don't show up…"

Gravel finally spoke. "It's rough when your cash cow gets out of the barn, ain't it?" And then he disconnected.

The phone rang again and again. "Don't answer it," Gravel said. "Screw him and feed him onions."

Addie found that terribly amusing and she laughed till she cried. Of course, she did have a buzz on.

"This call's from Cotton," I said as the phone rang again. Gravel took it.

"Cotton, you asshole. Where the hell have you been? I put on the biggest show in the history of the frickin' world, and you didn't even show up. I ought to' fire your ass right now." It was a threat he'd made many times before.

"My mother was in the hospital on her deathbed," Cotton said. "She passed away during the concert, Gravel. It was the worst possible timing, but what hell was I supposed to do?"

23

"Well, I'm really sorry for your loss, but ya could have at least called me," Gravel said. "You tellin' me your phone don't work in the hospital?"

"I tried to call you, but I kept getting that *All Circuits Busy* message. I guess the phone systems were overloaded with 1.2 million people calling and texting--" Cotton's voice began to rise with a positive inflection as he attempted, as any good manager will, to shift the focus back onto his narcissistic client. "Incredibly impressive, Gravel. Biggest crowd of all time came to New York City to see my main man, Gravel Gold. That's sweet, brother, real sweet."

"It *was* one hell of a show. Guess you'll have to buy the DVD," Gravel laughed.

"Where are you now?" Cotton asked.

"On the road."

"That's not much of an answer. There are a lot of roads in the world, Gravel."

"Bye, Cotton. And I really am sorry 'bout yer Mom," Gravel said and then disconnected. To Addie and me he said, "I guarantee ya Jimmy Bolen put him up to callin' just to try and find out where we are. Well, they'll know soon enough."

Our cell phones continued to chirp and buzz, until, eventually, we simply turned them off.

5

The mountains of Pennsylvania were beautiful in the fall, but not in the eyes of Gravel Gold. "I'll take the good 'ol Louisiana swamp or the wide open Texas plains any day a' the week," he said, staring out the window at the passing scenery. "All these mountains just look like great big turds to me."

I watched Gravel in the rearview mirror as I drove, as he and Addie got high on marijuana, whiskey, and amphetamines, the diet pills that Addie ate like candy. I knew more about Gravel Gold than just about anyone else in the world did, and for some reason, and in some odd way, I felt sorry for him. To me it seemed like the higher he got, the lower he looked.

Gravel went on, "Girl, didja know I was born way back in the Cajun swamp?" A stoned and blurry-eyed Addie shook her head no.

"I was raised by a single dad in a double wide atop three-high cinderblocks near a four-way stop on the outskirts of Shreveport, Louisiana." He paused to grin at his own word-play. "My daddy's name was Henry John Lamartiniere. And let me tell ya, we was white trash through and through. Don't remember nothin' 'bout my mama. She ran off when I was baby. But now look at me…I am the king of the whole damn world. The king."

Gravel turned quiet and sucked hard on a joint. The only sound was the low growl of the White Ford Bronco.

"Only person ever really loved me was my great-aunt. She took care of me sometimes when I was just a little kid, times when I didn't have nobody else. She was as fine a woman as there's ever been..."

I could've sworn there were tears in Gravel's eyes.

"*I* love you," Addie said and stroked his dark locks. "Trotter and I both love you, don't we, Trotter? And your wife, Gigi...she loves you, right? And think of all your fans--"

Gravel heard none of it. He rambled on sadly, "My daddy was a real piece 'a work. I don't know...I guess the sumbitch tried his best. Only taught me four things – how to drink, how to fight, how to drink, and how to fight. Now, look at me...the frickin' king of the frickin' world... king..."

When Addie and I tried to lift Gravel's spirits after that, he just waved us off and shut down. So we drove on in silence for a while through the dark mountains, thick forests, rolling farmland, and scattered small towns of Pennsylvania.

We stopped in the tiny hamlet of State College, also known as Happy Valley, which seemed quite ironic considering the mood inside the Bronco. That evening, we slipped quietly into a ragged place called Pickles' Tap Room and hid in a shadowy corner. No one recognized us as I signed us up, as per Gravel's instructions, to take part in the open-mic night at the bar, using the names Richard and Burton. The fall semester was still a couple weeks away from beginning at Penn State, so the crowd was small, made up of a dozen college jocks and their girlfriends, and a smattering of old drunk men. Exactly the type of crowd Gravel wanted. In the span of about 24 hours, he and I went from an audience of 1.2 million down to less than fifty.

We took the stage surreptitiously when it was our turn, and Gravel stood in the shadows behind the

26

microphone. The bar was dark and he was wrapped in a trench coat, his black hat pulled low to his eyes. Gravel drawled, "One time when I was a boy, my daddy brought an eight-foot alligator into the trailer for me to wrestle. I kicked that reptile's ass, duct-taped its jaws shut, and broke its back."

Their curiosity aroused, the old men at the bar swiveled slowly around on their stools and peered at the two of us, newcomers to the small Pickles' Tap Room stage. One of the jocks laughed and yelled sarcastically, "Yeah, right. Sure you did, cowboy."

Gravel ignored him and said, "I joined the Marines a few years after that and they taught me to shoot a machine gun. Sounded sorta like this." He struck his guitar with fury and moved his hands like lightning over the strings and frets. I followed his lead. All hell broke loose.

The jocks and their girlfriends crowded around the stage in awe, holding up cell phones, capturing the action in pictures and on video. The room was electric, the entire audience caught up in the moment, shouting and screaming, urging us on. After only a couple of minutes, recognition dawned on one, then another. I heard someone shout, "Hey, that's Gravel Gold! That's him! That's really him!" Then they began to chant his name, fists pumping in the air. More people streamed into the room. I don't know where they came from, but they came pouring in like a flood, surging toward us in the tiny bar. The walls seemed to pulsate with energy and I wondered if the whole damn place might collapse.

Suddenly, Addie was at my side onstage, clinging to me and shouting at me. I could barely hear her, but I recognized the fear in her voice. "Trotter, Trotter! We've got to get out of here!"

She was right. Things were out of control. The crowd was almost on top of us. Somewhere in the middle, there was pushing and shoving, a scuffle that broke into a fight. People were screaming, chairs were being thrown, bottles were breaking, blood was flowing.

And then Gravel Gold did something that I still don't understand to this day. He stopped playing guitar and roared into the microphone, "I am the Cajun Voodoo Man!" His voice was other-worldly and the room went silent as everyone stopped dead in their tracks. Gravel pulled his long knife from his boot and held it over his head. The crowd was mesmerized as he brought the knife down slowly and cut a six-inch gash in his forearm. Blood poured out onto the heads of the fans closest to him. I saw two mesmerized, Gravel-worshipping girls open their mouths and drink his blood, tongues out, lapping it up as it fell.

Then Gravel held the knife out straight ahead, pointing through the crowd, and said, "Clear a path for the Cajun Voodoo Man. Clear a path now!" And they did. I couldn't believe my own eyes. The audience parted down the middle, like the Red Sea for Moses, and Gravel, Addie and I walked through on dry land.

No one followed us for several minutes. They stood silent and still as if completely hypnotized by some unknown power. We jumped into the White Ford Bronco and made our escape, with Gravel's hand dripping red like a bloody glove.

6

"Oh, my God. Oh, my God." That was all Addie could say for a while.

I grabbed a bottle of Absolut and chugged. Addie snatched the bottle from me and washed down a handful of amphetamines.

"Was that some crazy shit or what?" Gravel roared as he grabbed a fresh bottle of his own - Jim Beam, as usual. "Hell yeah, baby! That's life on the edge."

"Your arm! Oh, my God, you cut your arm open! Why did you do that?" Addie cried and stammered.

"That was some black magic from the swamp, little Ad. Cajun voodoo."

"Oh, my God, that was *so* awesome." Frantically, Addie peeled off her tee shirt – she was wearing a bra – and tore it into strips. "We've got to clean that up so it doesn't get infected." She washed Gravel's arm and proceeded to wrap it with the homemade bandages.

"Oh, I don't need none 'a that. Ain't nothin' but a little cut," Gravel protested, but made no real effort to stop her.

I chugged and watched, and I didn't much like what I saw.

"Girl, you make one helluva nurse," Gravel slurred. "Nice bedside manner too." He pulled her close and kissed her hard.

"Damn it, Gravel, what is your problem?" I shouted incredulously. "You know, I'm sitting right her. Keep your hands off her."

Gravel smiled slyly. "Didn't hear little Addie complainin' none. Of course, she never does."

"You are such a prick," I said. Angry, forgetting where I was, I stood up clumsily in anger, but banged my head hard on the roof of the Bronco. It hurt and made my eyes blur for a moment. Or was it the half bottle of vodka I'd gulped?

Gravel laughed loudly. "Better have our sweet little nurse bandage that up too."

Addie leaned across the seat, slung one arm around my neck, and gently stroked my goat chin hair. "You okay, Trotter?"

I mumbled something, pulled away from her, and took another big swig.

"Be quiet," Gravel said, suddenly turning very serious. "I heard somethin'."

"What was it?" Addie asked. "I didn't hear anything."

Gravel put a finger to her lips to quiet her, and we listened to the silent night.

We were parked in a dark, secluded spot on a dirt road a couple of miles from town. There were no houses in view, no other vehicles, and only the moon casting its eerie glow on our drunkenness, and on the foggy, black night that surrounded the white Bronco. We peered out the windows of the vehicle into the thick, shadowy trees and bushes massed upon the turds of God, and saw nothing.

I could've sworn I could hear Addie's heart pounding, but then I realized it was my own, blood rushing in my ears.

Then came a whisper, "Gravel...Gravel Gold." It was a woman's voice, strained and frightful, as though she was speaking from beyond the grave. Almost like my dead mother's voice.

"Where did that come from?" I whispered, looking from side to side around the vehicle.

Suddenly, a woman's face slammed against the glass of the driver's side window. I jumped with a start and hit my head on the roof again, but no one laughed this time.

"Oh, God!" Addie shouted, her voice catching in her throat with a sob of terror.

The woman's hair was long, dirty blonde and twisted in knots. Her face was gray and maniacal. She raised a gun and pointed it at Gravel. "Get out," she hissed. "Please, get out, Gravel. Please."

Time moved like sap in a cold tree as the woman held the pistol with both hands trembling. Addie's eyes were big as a politician's lie. A wisp of cloud kissed the moon. Gravel turned his head toward me and winked. I swear to God, he winked.

"Okay, okay, I'm getting' out," he said softly. He stood in front of the woman and put his hands casually in his pockets. They stared at each other for a long moment.

"I sure do like those earrings," Gravel said. His voice was tender like a pricey filet.

The woman was caught off guard by the remark, and put one hand up to her ear, a crazy smile on her lips. "I got these at Target. I knew you'd like them."

"You were right about that. They make ya look real pretty."

The woman gripped the gun again with both hands. "I love you, Gravel Gold…I love you more than anything… but I have to shoot you."

"Why you wanna do somethin' like that?"

"Because you married that whore, that Gigi woman. You betrayed me. You and I were meant to be together."

"What? No, no, sweetie, that's all just made-up stuff for those tabloids," Gravel purred. "I don't really have a

31

wife; I'm single. And I've been lookin' for *you*."

Confusion played on the crazy woman's face as her eyes darted back and forth, as if answers and clarity might be lurking somewhere in the dark trees around us.

"Is that true?" she asked, pleadingly. "Is that really true?"

"Honey-pot, why else would I be all the way up here in your little home town?"

The woman wavered and muttered, "Well...well, I don't know..."

"Didn't you write me some letters?" Gravel guessed, speaking softly and soothingly, as he moved slowly toward her.

"Yes, yes, I wrote you a lot of letters. You read them?!"

"I sure did. They were beautiful, sweetie, they truly were. I told myself I just had to come up here to Pennsylvania and find you."

The woman's face softened and tears trickled down her cheeks. "Oh, Gravel," she said.

"Now, come on, give me that gun," Gravel whispered. "You and me got plenty to talk about, but we can't do it if you're pointin' that gun in my face."

"Oh, oh, my, yes, you're right," the woman mumbled as if a heavy weight was being lifted from her shoulders. Slowly, her arms went down until the gun was pointed at the Pennsylvania sod.

Gravel pulled the gun away from her in a flash and stuck it in his pocket. "You won't be needin' that anymore," he said.

The woman flung herself at Gravel and collapsed against his chest. Trembling, she looked up at him sheepishly with a sad, pathetic smile. "Oh, Gravel, this is the day I've dreamed about, the moment I've –"

Angrily, Gravel pulled away from the woman, slapped her hard across the face, and sent her sprawling to the ground. He seethed, "You are out of your freakin' psycho mind, trailer trash."

"But…what…please…I don't…" the woman pleaded.

"You stalked us with a gun out here in the middle of the night. You pointed it in my face and threatened to kill me and my friends. And now you think we're just gonna all of a sudden be nicety-nice, boyfriend-girlfriend? You must be dumber than a clump a' dirt."

The woman sobbed as Gravel's hulkish six-foot-four frame loomed over her. "I ought to beat the snot out of you. You're no different from that psycho bitch that stabbed George Harrison or that worthless bastard who shot John Lennon. People like you make me sick."

I wasn't sure what he might do next, and I didn't want to find out. I jumped out of the Bronco and tried to pull Gravel away from the woman. "Come on, man, leave her be. Let's just get out of here."

"Get yer hands off me," Gravel snapped.

Addie stepped quickly in front of Gravel and poked a finger in his chest. "You listen to me right now, Gravel Gold," she said firmly. "You march yourself over there and get in the car."

The angry rock star looked down at her and a huge grin spread across his face. "Or what?"

"Or I'll kick you right in the groin."

Gravel tipped his head back and roared with laughter. Then he went straight to the Bronco, lit up a cigarette, and leaned against the side panel. "Life with Gravel Gold ain't ever boring, is it little Addie? You know, this kinda thing don't happen to most people."

Neither I nor Addie had a response to that. We just stood in place as if frozen there, watching and waiting as the woman whimpered on the ground. Gravel drew hard on his fag and studied the stars for several very long minutes.

Finally, he asked, "What's your name?"

33

"Wh—what? Me?" the woman muttered. "Cynthia, my name's Cynthia."

Gravel nodded slowly and blew out smoke. "Cynthia," he said softly. "Get up on your feet and come over here."

Addie and I made wide eyes at each other, having no idea what Gravel was up to.

The woman whimpered, "But…please….I'm sorry, please don't hurt me. I just…"

"Stand up and come over here."

"Gravel, what are--" I began.

"Shut up, Trotter," Gravel said, cutting me off, as the strange woman rose and moved toward him. "Now you listen to me, Cynthia. You need help, you know that? And you're gonna get some help, aren't you?"

The woman nodded meekly. "Yes, yes, I will."

"Promise me. Swear it," Gravel commanded, his voice strong yet surprisingly tender.

The woman looked almost as though she'd somehow fallen into some sort of trance. "I promise…I promise you I will. I swear it."

We drove the woman to her house, but before Gravel let her out of the car, he stuffed a huge wad of hundred dollar bills in her jacket pocket.

Addie and I stared in disbelief. When I started to open my mouth, Gravel looked at me coldly and said, "Shut up, Trotter. Shut up and drive."

7

We reached Pittsburgh by dawn, where one of Gravel's private jets was waiting to take him back to Nashville. Though Gravel didn't particularly like it, Addie and I opted to drive back so that we could spend a little quiet time alone along the way. None of us knew it at the time, but a firestorm had been ignited by our impromptu show in Happy Valley. In just six hours, dozens of videos of Gravel Gold slicing his arm and calling himself 'The Cajun Voodoo Man' already had millions of YouTube views. It seemed as though everyone in the world was talking and tweeting about it.

Addie and I took our time returning to Music City, stopping here and there along the way, maintaining 'radio silence' with cell phones off, and stretching a nine-hour drive into nearly two days. When we reached Gravel's mansion in Franklin, south of Nashville after midnight the following day, the front security gate was open, there were few cars in the drive, and the house was mostly dark. This was surprising because Gravel's mansion was usually the scene of raucous all-night parties.

"Where is everybody?" Addie whispered.

"Maybe the Rapture happened," I joked.

"I didn't know Satan had a Rapture of his own," Addie giggled.

We slipped quietly inside and stood for a moment in the dim light of the foyer. Nothing appeared to have changed while we'd been gone. Gravel's stuffed, six-foot alligator still posed threateningly on the teak wood table with its teeth glimmering and mouth forever open. Gravel's favorite picture - a ten-foot tall poster of himself riding a palomino stallion onstage in London - still hung on the big wall beside the grand, spiral staircase. And his most prized items - the official NFL football from the Super Bowl where Gravel did the halftime show, and a New Orleans Saints helmet signed by every member of the team – remained undisturbed inside the tall, glass display cabinet.

As we started up the marble stairs to the second floor, Gravel's voice emanated ominously from the kitchen, "That you, Gigi?"

Addie and I froze mid-step, looked at each other, and I raised my eyebrows.

"I *said*..." his voice was stronger now and angry. "Is that you, Gigi? You better answer me, bitch."

"Gravel," I said quickly. "It's me, Trotter...and Addie's with me."

"Get yer asses in here now," Gravel demanded.

Arrogant jerk.

We entered the kitchen where Gravel Gold sat tilted back in his plush velvet recliner, feet up, a bottle of Jim Beam between his legs, and a shotgun resting in the crook of his arm, pointed our direction.

"Where have you been, Trotter?" Gravel asked. "And why didn't you answer my calls?"

"We just got, um, sidetracked along the way...and my phone died," I said. It wasn't entirely a lie - my phone was dead...now.

"Bullshit!" Gravel snapped, raising the gun just a bit. "When I leave you a message, I expect an answer. We got a whole new batch of songs to work on. I don't know whether to fire you or shoot you."

"Gravel, please put the gun away," Addie interceded. "We've been driving all day. We're tired and just want to get some sleep."

There was a long, uncomfortable silence as Gravel studied us. Finally, I realized he wasn't really seeing us, but rather, seemed to be looking through us. He was very drunk and strangely distracted. Finally, he spoke, "That little whore is runnin' around on me."

Hello, kettle…it's the pot.

"Can't prove nothin' yet, but I think maybe she's got somethin' serious goin' with some actor from that movie she's been workin' on. I don't give a rat's ass if she picks up a little young action every once in a while for fun, but this kinda shit ain't gonna fly. No, sir, ain't gonna happen. I'll shoot her when she walks in that door. I'll shoot her right in the head."

"Gravel, think it through," I said. "You don't really want to do that."

"The hell I don't."

"Even *you* can't kill your wife and get by with it," I said. "They'll put you away for life, man. You got records to make and concerts to play, right? Forget about Gigi. Divorce her, cut her off, but don't shoot her."

"Trotter's right, Gravel. Listen to him," Addie said softly, pleadingly. "It won't do you any good to shoot her. Just give me the gun. Give it to me."

Gravel stared up at Addie from his recliner, and ran his hand roughly over his face. "Aahh, maybe you're right," he said wearily.

Addie took the shotgun gingerly from him and handed it to me. I placed it surreptitiously in a nearby closet.

"You look tired," Addie said to Gravel. "Why don't you get some sleep? Things will look different in the morning."

Gravel took Addie's hand and pulled her down to sit on the arm of the chair next to him. "You're a good girl,

Addie. You know that? A real good girl." He patted her thigh and left his hand there, then kissed her on the cheek.

Addie pulled herself away gently and said, "You've had too much to drink. Go to bed and get some sleep."

"How 'bout you come tuck me in," Gravel said as he struggled up out of the chair and staggered across the kitchen. "Come on, give me a little company tonight." He put a big arm around Addie's tiny waist, teetering as drunks often do, with one shuffle step forward in place, one step back.

"Uh, she's sleeping with me, Gravel," I said.

Gravel looked at me through glassy eyes, with an expression that suggested he'd forgotten I was even in the room. "Now, why would this sweet little thing want to be with you when she could be with Gravel Gold, the new King of the music world?" He clumsily tried to smooth Addie's hair with affection, and kissed her on top of the head.

"Just leave her alone," I said more strongly.

"Kiss my ass."

Addie pulled away from Gravel just as Gigi entered the room, having come in a side entrance while the three of us were engaged in conversation. Gravel immediately focused fully on his wife and away from us.

Saved by the Birmingham belle.

Gigi had big blonde hair like Pamela Anderson, and a similar body, although slightly more straight and narrow, like a model, and not quite as full and curvy as Pamela's. Gigi perched atop steep, neon green high heels that matched her miniskirt, and when she walked, she reminded me of a nervous stork in shallow water. In spite of her sometimes abrasive way, I liked Gigi for the most part. She basically meant well even though she was a little rough around the edges, just a backwoods country girl from Alabama trying to fit into a high society world. She wore far too much makeup for my taste, enough to make the moon look like Mars; and like some nightmarish conglomeration of trailer park glitterati and blinding bling, she wore enough jewelry to embarrass even Elizabeth Taylor, Lil Jon and Nelly.

Completely oblivious to the pre-existing mood of the room, Gigi started in full bore with her high-pitched voice, "Ya'll ain't gonna believe what happened to me tonight. I'm at this bar, see, and there's these two skinny little skanks wearin' like, shit from Wal-Mart, and they're like givin' me all these dirty looks, and I'm like, hey, what the hell's your problem? And then all of a sudden, they get all up in my face with a real bad attitude. So I flip 'em the bird. Then one of them calls me fat. Fat! Can you believe that?"

Gigi raised her top and proudly displayed her smooth stomach and perfect, bare breasts. "Do you see any fat in here? Hell, no, you don't see no fat in here."

Gigi rolled back into her story, chattering like a shopping cart rolling backwards down a hill, "So I look at this one skank, and I'm like, hey girl, you *wish* you had some a' this. And then you know what that bitch did? She smacks me right in the face. Right here. See it? It's still red." She poked repeatedly at her cheek to make sure we saw the exact spot.

"So I'm like, listen here, girls, I'm gonna beat me some bitches up. And I told her, that's the last time you're gonna smack somebody's face. Then I yanked the one girl by the hair and punched the other one right in the mouth."

Gigi held out the back of her hand for us to inspect. "Look, look here at my knuckles. See that? I cut my hand on her teeth."

Then she rolled on like a freight train with no pause between syllables or sentences, "And when I hit her she falls back against the bar, and she's all crying and spittin' blood, and then their boyfriend comes over, and I'm like, hey, pretty boy, you want some 'a this too? And then all of a sudden, security grabs me and drags me outta there. I told 'em, I said, do you know who the hell I am? My husband is *Gravel Gold*. Gravel Gold's gonna come back down here and kick every one of your asses. Now ain't that some bullshit, if you ever heard it?"

Gigi finally stopped to catch her breath. She opened the refrigerator, her back to us, and leaned in, bent at the waist, and her very short skirt rode up to reveal the full length of her shapely legs and the bottom of her buttocks. The room was dead silent for a long moment as we watched her remove a kiwi strawberry juice box from the fridge, poke the straw through the top, and begin to suck, her luscious, red lips wrapped around the tiny white stick.

"What?" she said. "What are ya'll looking at?"

Finally, Gravel collapsed into his recliner with uncontrollable laughter.

"You think it's *funny*?" she asked him. "Some skank says I'm fat and you think it's funny?"

"Come here, you crazy, sexy woman," Gravel said, as he pulled her into the chair on top of him, and buried his face in her ample bosom. Addie and I seized the golden opportunity and slipped out of the room unnoticed.

8

The following day at four in the afternoon there was a roar. A very serious, bone-rattling roar.

Addie and I leapt to our feet and rushed out into the upper hall. "What in the world was that?" Addie said, her voice trembling.

"I don't know," I replied. "I've never heard anything like it in my life."

Eyes and ears alert, we tiptoed carefully along the hallway, crept down the stairs, and peeked around the corner into the mansion's great hall on the main floor. Neither of us could believe our eyes.

There was a huge male lion with a spectacular mane lounging on the mauve davenport.

The great cat had a heavy collar around its neck, and attached to the collar was a long, chain-link leash. At the end of the leash was Gigi Gold, sprawled on the Fereghan Sarouk carpet in the foyer.

I stopped on the bottom stair and Addie hid behind me, peeking over my shoulder at the beast on the sofa. "Oh, my God," she whispered.

The lion gazed our direction with little interest, its eyes half-closed, its tongue lolling partly out of its mouth between very large teeth.

Gravel Gold was standing in the hallway with a turkey sandwich in one hand, and a .357 magnum in the other.

"Gigi, where the hell did that animal come from?" he asked, his voice even, his pistol trained on the lion.

"Don't you dare shoot my baby!" Gigi shrieked, scrambling to her feet and throwing her arms around the big cat's neck.

Gravel didn't move a muscle. "What...the hell...is that damn animal...doin' in my house?" he said slowly, through clenched teeth and bits of bread.

"You told me I could have a cat," Gigi said. She stood up and put her hands defiantly on her hips.

"A cat," Gravel said. "Not a friggin' lion."

None of us had noticed the man and woman standing in the foyer. "No, no, no, no, no," the man said, shaking his head vigorously and making a stop signal with his palms out toward us. "Absolutely no guns around Larry."

"Who the hell is Larry?" Gravel asked, his voice rising. "And who in God's name are you people?"

Gigi, you got some 'splainin' to do.

"Larry is my lion," Gigi said. "And these here are Larry's trainers. They're gonna move in with us and help me take care of him. Ain't that sweet of them?"

Gravel cocked his head slightly to the right with a perplexed look on his face.

Gigi began to cajole Gravel. "Oh, baby, baby," she said, kicking into her natural accelerated speech mode. "You told me I could get a cat. You promised me I could. And just look at him – he's so gentle and so beautiful." Gigi turned toward me and Addie, looking for moral support. "Ain't he beautiful?" she asked.

Addie slid down behind me and I stuttered, "Oh, yeah, he's uh, he's something. He's really something."

Gigi moved to Gravel's side and wrapped her arms around him, but he just kept staring at the big cat on the couch. Gigi rambled on, "Oh, Gravel, Larry won't be no trouble. Besides, I'll be workin' on the Itty Bitty commercials with him. That's how I got him – from the

Itty Bitty cat food people. See, we shot some of the commercials today with me and Larry, and I, like, just totally fell in love with him. I told 'em I wanted to take him home with me so I could get more comfortable with him, you know. And they're all like, hey, we can't allow that, and I'm like, 'Hey, what if I buy him from the company?' And they said Larry had to have his caretakers with him, like, at all times, and I said 'Okay, I'll buy them too.' So I did." Gigi stopped to catch her breath.

Gravel looked from the cat to the caretakers. The woman was tall and reed-thin with frizzy blonde hair. "Hello, Mr. Gold," she said. "My name's Beverly Cox. I raised Larry from the time he was a little cub, and he's generally a very sweet-natured cat, unless something disturbs him."

"And I'm Dr. Richard Marks, formerly a lion expert with the San Diego Zoo," the man said. He was an older gentleman with leathery, tanned skin and a pencil-thin moustache. "The cat food company contracted me as a consultant on this marketing project," Mr. Marks continued. "While this arrangement of your wife's is a bit unorthodox, I feel confident that Beverly and I will be up to the task of integrating Larry into your home."

"Gonna need one heck of a litter box," I whispered to Addie.

"She must've totally paid them a fortune," Addie whispered back.

Gravel still hadn't responded. He'd simply let everyone say their piece while he resumed eating his sandwich. Finally, he spoke. "No."

"No what?" Gigi said, her voice shooting even higher than its normal screeching pitch.

"No. No. No," Gravel said.

Gigi straightened her back and stuck out her chin. "Okay, then," she said. "Larry and I will sleep on the

43

bus." She tugged gently on the lion's chain. "Come on, Larry," Gigi said. "Let's go out to the bus." The cat did not stir.

"Up, Larry," Beverly said, and the lion got up from the davenport and followed them toward the front door.

"*Bus?*" Gravel suddenly said. "What bus?"

"I bought a bus," Gigi said matter-of-factly, turning to face Gravel. "*You* have tour buses, right? So I bought one for me. I need one."

Once again, Gravel had that dumbfounded look on his face. "Why do you need a bus?"

"I'm going on the road for the Itty Kitty Cat Food promos."

Gravel started to speak, but held himself in check. Wheels were turning in his head.

"They want me to do a tour of their major markets," Gigi continued. "They like my style." She shook her hair back, obviously full of herself. "I'll make appearances, sing their jingle, and sign autographs. It'll be fun and I'll make a lot of money as the new spokesperson for the Itty Kitty Cat Food Company."

Standing in the foyer, Gigi suddenly slipped into her spokesperson pose and persona, and pretended to be holding up a can of the product for a make-believe camera. In her best television voice, she said, "Itty Bitty Cat Food - it's the perfect kitty food for *your* itty bitty kitty, no matter what size he is." Then she pointed at the cat as smoothly as Vanna White points at letters on Wheel of Fortune.

9

After Beverly put Larry in his cage, Gigi gave all of us the full bus tour. We followed behind, making the appropriate oohs and aahs about the vehicle's elaborate features. Gravel simply rubbed his three day whiskers and shook his head. He'd married Gigi for the extra dose of excitement she could bring to his life, and this was a banner day – a lion and a multi-million-dollar bus in one swoop.

The bus had eight televisions, three satellite systems, X-boxes, PlayStations, a tanning bed, a pet area, a full kitchen, a walk-in shower for three, marble fixtures, silk sheets, and the finest leather upholstery on the chairs and couches. It even had an expandable section to increase the living area when the bus was parked. It was a Ritz-Carlton on wheels.

"Looky here, Gravel baby," Gigi said excitedly. "It's got a rhinestone grill. We can grill us up some fine steaks and pork chops riding down the highway. Ooh, come see this!" Gigi ran to the master bath like a little girl on Christmas morning. We followed close behind. Again she struck her Vanna White pose. "Taa daa, a rhinestone toilet!"

"Alright, everybody off the bus," Gravel said abruptly. "Everybody but me and Gigi."

We did as he said. Outside, Addie asked, "What was that about?"

"I'm not sure," I answered.

"He sounded angry. Do you think he'll hurt her?"

Inside, Gravel had his hands on Gigi, but definitely not to hurt her. He ripped her leopard-print dress off her shapely body, and kissed and caressed her from head to toe, pausing here and there to lavish additional attention upon specific areas of interest. As he did so, Gigi dug her neon green fingernails into the back of his neck, and pushed his head in so hard and tight he thought he'd suffocate.

Gravel came up gasping for air. "Lord, woman," he said. "I guess if a man's gotta be smothered, might as well be down in the sweet spot."

Gravel and Gigi made love on the leather couches, the marble countertops, and the majestic Teak wood and Mpingo dining table. Then they did it on the top bunk, worked their way down to the bottom bunk, and eventually the floor. Finally, with Gravel enthroned upon the rhinestone toilet, Gigi bounced up and down on the Gold Member, and pounded him like a butcher pounds meat on the chop block.

"Ya know, ya really do piss me off sometimes," he moaned as she rode him. "But ya surely do know how to drive me wild, too."

Straddling Gravel with her hands on his shoulders, Gigi arched her back and shuddered so violently it seemed to shake the entire bus. At last, panting and sweating, Gigi collapsed against Gravel's wide, muscular chest and snuggled in close to him.

"Baby, I do love it when ya give me the golden shower," Gravel said with a husky, sex-infused voice. "Ya got a whole lotta crazy goin' on inside your head."

Gigi nuzzled Gravel's ear and whispered, "So, now can I keep the bus? Please, can I, sweetie?"

Gravel smiled and groaned slowly, "Well, now...I guess maybe...just maybe, you've earned it."

46

"Baby, ain't no maybe about it," Gigi purred. "And what about the cat?"

"What *about* the cat?" Gravel asked.

"Please, can I keep it, please?" she whined with pouty lips, drawing the last word out for nearly ten full seconds.

"Think about it, Gigi," Gravel argued. "How can we keep an animal like that inside the mansion? A gator's one thing – I can handle them – but I ain't never wrestled a damn lion. And I don't think I'd wanna try."

Gigi gripped Gravel's face and kissed him hotly on the mouth, her tongue plunging in and probing. "Please," she whispered softly. "Let me keep him."

"But there'd be huge piles of cat crap all ov--"

Gigi again cut off his words with another passionate kiss and began to stroke him. "I promise I'll never ask for nothin' ever again."

"Damn it, Gigi," Gravel closed his eyes and moaned. "You're a real pain in the ass sometimes."

"Pretty please?"

"Alright, alright, you can keep it," Gravel acquiesced. "But it better not eat anybody."

10

The following Saturday night, Gravel
Gold threw a party and hundreds of guests filled the
mansion to overflowing. They were an eclectic mix of
characters – Gravel wouldn't have it any other way –
including hip-hop singers, rock musicians, eccentric
novelists, bean counters and all the higher-ups from the
record label, X-treme sports stars, NFL players, fighter
pilots, some regular folks from Gravel's favorite local
pub, and a lion. The only one missing was Gigi. She was
performing at the Grand Ol' Opry up on the northeast side
of Nashville, and would be late to the festivities.

Jazz Bolen was the most beautiful woman at the party
and maybe in the world, an honest to God seventeen on a
scale of one to ten. Her mother was from Madrid and her
father from Reykjavik, and her eyes shimmered with an
other-worldly luminescence like the Spanish sun on the
crystal blue of Glacier Bay. A slinky black cocktail gown
clung to her breasts and hips while wisps of dirty blonde
hair teased the corners of her pouty mouth. She was
Jimmy Bolen's wife, but Gravel Gold had decided he had
to have her, at least once.

Jazz's phone buzzed inside her tiny clutch purse and
she surreptitiously checked it. It was a one-word text
message that read: BUS. Gravel Gold rarely messaged
anyone, but in this particular instance, he was moderately
drunk and highly motivated by unbridled sexual desire.

Jazz felt a tingle between her legs and bit her bottom lip nervously, excitedly as she deleted the message. After rapidly downing her glass of chardonnay, she slipped casually and carefully away from her husband and through the crowd, working her way toward a rear exit.

Gravel was waiting for her on the bus, Gigi's bus, and when Jazz tapped lightly on the door, he pulled her quickly inside without a word spoken between them. The span of Gravel's large hands reached almost fully around Jazz's tiny waist as he hoisted her high over his head and then lowered her to himself. She wrapped her tanned legs tightly around him, cupped his face in her hands, and they kissed, tongues pressed together, searching, probing, finding.

The bus was silent but for their breathing as they separated and undressed. Gravel laid Jazz on the master bed and roamed over her naked body, loving it with his tongue and lips. She returned the favor, gently and deliberately, up and down, round and round. Finally, he stopped her, pulled away, and lay on his back on the bed.

Jazz dipped her head slightly, grinning like the Cheshire cat, her long, thick locks swaying before her as she crawled up the bed toward him on all fours, rubbing her breasts along his thighs. Finally, she slid herself down onto his hardness, slowly, like butter melting and sliding over hot pancakes. Then she went wild.

Back inside the mansion, everyone, *everyone* was watching television. The same sordid program was showing on all thirty flat screens throughout the house. No one ate, drank or spoke. We were all transfixed by the images of Gravel Gold and Jazz Bolen having sex on the big screen TVs. Every single moment, every single movement had been captured by the bus' hidden security cameras, and broadcast directly via a live feed into the mansion's video system.

49

That was when I realized that Gigi wasn't nearly as stupid as she pretended to be; she could be quite conniving when necessary. Claiming a headache, Gigi had skipped her final turn onstage and come home early from the Grand Ol' Opry, much to the dismay of the Opry's host. In the driveway, she'd seen Gravel pull Jazz into the bus, and her headache had been replaced by a vengeful rage. She had then instructed her technical assistant to pull the security feed directly from the bus and deliver it live to all of the party's attendees via the televisions scattered throughout the mansion. Screens that moments before had been showing sports highlights, music videos, or news reports were suddenly broadcasting porn, live.

In the Gold Theater Room, Jimmy Bolen was grim, his jaw set hard, teeth clenched tightly, as he stood glaring at the images on the massive thirty-foot screen. A full, humiliating minute passed with no one daring to speak or move. Finally, Jimmy placed his drink carefully on a table, straightened his Salvatore Ferragamo tie, and walked out of the mansion with his eyes straight ahead, black as coal. His Jaguar roared off into the night.

Two very old and very drunk men were sitting near me. They were the first to speak and break the silence. One slurred loudly, "What channel is this?" The other said, "I don't know, but I guarantee it ain't the Hallmark channel."

Cotton Black had known Gravel Gold since Gravel first moved to Nashville, and he'd been his manager for almost ten years. During that time, Cotton had seen Gravel do a lot of stupid and outrageous things, but this turn of events left him stunned. He stared up at the images and muttered, "You stupid son of a bitch. You damn stupid ignorant son of a bitch."

I ran out to the bus and pounded on the door. "Gravel, Gravel," I shouted. "Open up!"

The door opened suddenly and Gravel stood there naked and proud, his erection still as hard as cedar. It was much more than I wanted to see. It was one thing to see his penis on a television screen, but having it pointed directly in my face was another thing entirely.

"What the hell's your problem?" he grumbled.

"You got trouble, big trouble," I said. "Gigi must know what's going on because I think she set you up. And Jimmy most definitely knows now."

Gravel didn't bother arguing or asking *knows what?* He could tell by my voice and behavior that something was up, and it wasn't just his cock.

Jazz appeared at the door. "Jimmy knows?" she said with great concern. "How? How could he know?"

I stepped inside the bus with them as they got dressed. "I hate to tell you this," I said. "But everybody knows. The bus apparently has hidden cameras. Gigi must've somehow had the video piped into the house. Everyone saw the two of you together."

"Shit," Gravel hissed. "That little bitch!"

He continued to rage, oblivious to Jazz and me, while pulling on his black, rhinestone-studded cowboy boots, buttoning up his rhinestone-smothered western shirt, knocking things over and breaking things, and cursing vehemently all the while. "I'm gonna kill that woman. I swear to God I'll kill her."

Outside, tires were squealing as cars left the lot in a hurry. At least half the guests were making a very quick exit, wanting no part of the trouble they sensed coming. The other half stayed behind, filled with anticipation as Gravel Gold strode up the walk and through the front door of the mansion. This was live entertainment at its best.

"Where's Gigi?" he demanded of the guests who remained.

Everyone remained silent, frozen in place.

51

"Where is she?" he screamed so loudly that it hurt my ears and rattled the chandelier.

Blister, the drummer, spoke up, "She left, Gravel. Took off a few minutes ago."

"Where'd she go?" Gravel asked.

"She didn't say a word. Just ran out of here like a crazy woman," Blister answered.

Gravel grabbed a bottle of bourbon from the bar and downed half of it. He stood in the middle of the living room and gazed around at the faces around him. A sinister smile formed ever so slowly on his face, his lips curling devilishly with that patented Gravel grin. Finally, he said, "Shit happens, don't it?"

There was some nervous laughter in the crowd and a few people mumbled words of agreement.

Gravel took another swig from the bottle and shouted, "This here's a party, ain't it? So let's party. Benji boy, crank the music back up. Keep the whiskey flowin'. I wanna see some folks enjoyin' themselves, or else get the hell out."

The party sprang quickly back to life. From the big screen, The Cars echoed through the mansion singing, *I know tonight she comes*. Gravel popped a few greenies – I recognized them as Addie's diet pills – from a bag in his pocket, and swaggered over to a trio of giggling blonde women. "Hey, pretty girls," he said, doing his best Ric Ocasek impression. "Who wants to come tonight?"

11

Gravel Gold was getting wasted and wound up at the same time, partying as only he could. The festivities had moved to the large front room and only about fifty guests remained. These were the truly dedicated partiers, ones who had a serious appetite for dangerous adventure or else were simply too drunk or high to have sense enough to leave. Swigging from a bottle of Absolut, I stood on the fringes with Addie and watched the proceedings unfold.

"I have a bad feeling," Addie said.

"Yeah, I got the same feeling," I replied. "Nothing good can come from any of this."

"I wonder sometimes if he's completely crazy," Addie said. "I mean, like, is he totally psycho?"

"He's been crazy as long as I've known him, which is about ten years," I said. "But it does seem like he's gotten more out of control in the last year or two. I guess it's true what they say about absolute power…"

Gravel was standing atop a large end table with his shirt off, wearing his black, rhinestone-studded cowboy hat and his .357 holstered on his hip. He was playing guitar, stomping the heel of his shiny, pointy-toed cowboy boot on the tabletop, and singing some outrageous, alternative thrash country number to the crowd's great delight.

Grandpa drank herbal tea,
For his aggression therapy,
He beat his dog with a cane,
He beat his wife with a chain,
He keep one hand in his pocket,
He don't believe in no rocket,
He keep two hands on the wheel,
His fantasy is surreal.
You better not look in his eyes,
You may not like what you see.
He got a bad case
Of salmonella sitcom disease.

Gravel leaped from the table, smashed his guitar into pieces, and said, "I say we let the cat outta the bag!"

He raced to the lion's cage – in spite of the strong objections from Linda's two caretakers – and threw open the door. "My money paid for the damn animal," he shouted. "It's my property and I can bring it out if I want to."

"No, you can't do this!" Beverly said.

"We will not be responsible for--" Dr. Marks began but Gravel cut him off.

"That's right," Gravel said. "You ain't responsible for nothing. So mind yer own damn business."

Larry the lion strode calmly into the room as the onlookers moved nervously away.

"Don't be afraid, folks," Gravel said. "It's just a big cat. Wouldn't hurt a fly."

As if on cue, Larry plopped down on the Persian rug in the middle of the room, taking it all in stride, alert but calm. I imagined he must be thinking, *Hey, if my ancestors and relatives can handle performing in circuses in front of thousands of humans, then I can handle this.*

"See what I mean?" Gravel continued, dishing out the bullshit in his own inimitable style. "Besides, I bet most of these folks ain't never been to a party with a lion before. We can't deny 'em the opportunity to see this beautiful creature in all its glory." Reluctantly, Beverly and Dr. Marks said nothing more, but they kept a watchful eye on the proceedings.

"Somebody fetch me a new guitar," Gravel said. One quickly appeared, and Gravel jumped back up on the table and into a new number. The three young blondes that he'd spoken to earlier gathered around, gazing up at him, pursing their lips and making eyes at him as he sang. They boldly ran their hands up and down his legs, and caressed his crotch through his rhinestone-studded jeans, bringing his manhood to full attention as he gyrated wildly and brought the song to a climactic end. Then he pulled his pistol from its holster and pointed it at the ceiling. As with so many bad things, it all happened in the blink of an eye.

Dr. Marks jumped up shouting, "No! I said no guns!" But it was too late. Gravel shouted, "Yee Haw!" and rapid-fired a number of random shots upward.

A few of the blasts hit the base of the ornate chandelier, severing the support rod, destroying the junction box and shorting out the wiring inside. This kicked a breaker and cut power to the room. The chandelier was left dangling by a single cord. There was a moment of chaos as our eyes adjusted to the dim light flowing in from adjacent rooms. Smoke hung in the air and small bits of plaster slipped loose and fell – some in chunks, some like a fine mist – onto the guests as the huge light fixture swung ever so slightly to and fro. The scene was absurd and surreal.

Larry was disoriented and frightened by the commotion, surrounded by humans, and saw no apparent avenue of escape. Snarling, he crouched low in a defensive posture in the middle of the room.

Suddenly the chandelier let loose and plummeted thirty feet from the high ceiling of the grand room. The massive fixture came down upon Larry with an ungodly crash, sending shards of glass and debris around the room and into the skin of bystanders. It broke the great cat's neck, killing it instantly.

Silence filled the room.

"Whoa," Gravel said finally. "Sorry 'bout that."

Screaming, Beverly crawled through the glass and debris, threw herself upon the lion, and wailed with sorrow. Dr. Marks rushed toward Gravel with fury, pointing his knobby finger, wanting desperately to strike the big man before him, but not daring to.

"You imbecile!" he screamed. "I warned you that there must be no guns around Linda. Now look what you've done!"

Someone called 9-1-1 and soon there were sirens in the distance.

"The police will be here any minute," Dr. Marks said. "They will put you in your place, Mr. Gold. You are going to regret this day."

The poor doctor is suffering from delusions.

"The police? What the hell we need the police for?" Gravel said incredulously. "It's just a cat. A big cat, for sure...but still, just a cat. I'm truly sorry 'bout what happened and all, but, I mean, really, what's the big deal?"

"You've killed a prized and cherished animal," Dr. Marks said. "And you discharged a weapon here in the house, endangering us all."

"And it's my damn house," Gravel roared back. "I got the right to shoot my guns in my house if I want to, you little shit. This here's still the United States of America."

"You are a dangerous lunatic," Dr. Marks said. You have injured innocent people, and could have killed someone."

"Alright, maybe a couple people got cut by a little broken glass. Wouldn't be a real party without a little blood. I got plenty of ointment and bandages in the supply room. You're makin' a big deal outta' nothin', Marks."

"Making a big deal out of nothing?" Dr. Marks was incredulous. "Just look around. You call this nothing?"

"Just another party where I come from," Gravel said with a shrug.

Several of the partiers had captured the entire debacle on their video cameras and cell phones, and soon the images and events of the evening were uploaded and spread around the globe – Gravel singing on the table, the blondes rubbing his pelvic region, the sounds of gunfire, the crashing chandelier, shards of glass in a smoky room, and one big, dead lion. All of it coming right on the heels of the Happy Valley fiasco.

They say there's no such thing as bad publicity, but I'm not so sure.

By the time the police and paramedics arrived, there were only about twenty guests still in the house. Most of them had slipped quietly away beforehand, not wanting to get involved in the messy events that were sure to follow. Those that remained were either passed out or were the sort of people who always relished being a part of messy events.

Gravel's statement to the police was classic Gold. "Officers, this whole thing was just one big unfortunate accident. I had no idea that gun was loaded. I was just jokin' 'round with my friends. Pointed the damn thing at the ceiling and it went off and hit the chandelier. Nobody was more shocked or devastated than me, I promise ya that, officers."

Gravel rubbed his forehead and eyes wearily for dramatic effect. He sighed deeply and continued, "I'll tell ya, I'm terribly upset by this whole incident. I'm real sorry about the cat. He was such a sweet thing. We loved that animal like it was our own child. Damn, it's gonna break poor Gigi's heart when she finds out."

"Where is your wife, Mr. Gold? May we speak with her?" one investigator asked.

"She sang at the Opry tonight and then went out with some friends. Hard to say when she'll get home," Gravel answered. "But you're welcome to talk to her anytime."

The officers took statements from everyone, and the paramedics tended to those who'd been hurt by flying glass. Fortunately for Gravel, their injuries were minor, they declined to be taken to the emergency room, and none of them seemed prone to take legal action against him at the moment.

At 3:00 am, the authorities removed the lion's body from the scene, wrapped up their investigation and allowed everyone to go home. Beverly Cox, still dazed and dabbing her eyes with tissues, was given permission to ride with Larry's remains back to the animal control center. Dr. Marks wrapped a blanket around Beverly and escorted her outside. As they left the mansion, the good doctor pointed his bony finger at Gravel one last time and uttered a solemn warning: "I assure you, Mr. Gold, you have not heard the last of this. You will pay for what you have done."

12

Downstairs, Gravel had run off almost everyone, including the guests, the servants, and our band mates. Only the three blondes remained. He'd taken them to the master bedroom suite, instructed them to get comfortable, and promised to join them later.

Addie went to bed, but I was too wired to sleep. The sun was coming up on a new day, and I decided to start it with some serious drinking. I found my bottle of Absolut and joined Gravel and Jim Beam at the kitchen bar. We toasted the sunrise like the dearest of old friends, like twin planets with a common orbit now about to be sucked into a black hole.

"Trotter, you ever think about dyin'?" Gravel asked, suddenly serious and reflective.

"Yeah, sometimes."

"Does it scare ya?"

Where did this come from and where is it going? I wondered, rubbing my aching neck.

"Dyin's the great mystery, the great unknown," Gravel said. "When we come kickin' and screamin' into this world, dyin's the one and only thing we know for sure is comin'. But it's the one damn thing we know the least about. Ain't that some weird shit?"

"Here's to weird shit," I said, and did a double shot. "I think it's the unknown that scares us a lot more than dying does."

"Most folks, yeah," Gravel said. "But I love the unknown. Bring it on. Bring it the hell on." He knocked his glass to mine and we downed another.

"I promise ya this," Gravel continued. "You'll never see me wastin' away in a nursin' home, hooked up to a bunch a' machines, or in a wheelchair totin' around an oxygen tank. None 'a that crap for me. I plan t' die like I live – hard and fast. Worse comes t' worse, I'll do the Hemingway thing. Give me the bang, not the whimper."

"Here's to the bang," I said, and we drank again.

"Let me show ya somethin', Trotter." Gravel led me to the bedroom and cracked the door just enough for us to peek in on three blonde angels snuggled together in his massive bed. "Now there's the real bang," Gravel said as he closed the door quietly.

We took our bottles out onto the patio and sat on the marble floor to watch the morning sky streak orange and red over the Tennessee countryside. *Red sky at morning, sailors take warning*, ran through my brain. Gently rolling hills stretched off in a beeline toward Birmingham, a hundred and seventy-five miles dead south.

"Let me ask you something," I said.

"Shoot."

"Why'd you marry her?"

Gravel laughed. "Hell, there's a question for the ages," he said. "Guess 'cause I hadn't never done it before. Gotten married, that is."

I smiled crookedly at him and raised my glass. "Here's to dumbass decisions," I said.

He clinked his glass to mine in agreement and we got a little bit drunker.

"Gigi knew the deal when she married me," Gravel said. "She and I had an understanding, and truth is, it kinda turned her on. We had plenty 'a threesomes and foursomes and I never heard her complainin' none. If she wants to be married to me, she got to learn t' take the good with the bad. Everybody knows rock stars don't play that monogamy game."

He paused to refill his glass before continuing. "What about you? Seems like you're getting' yourself all tangled up in knots over that screwy little Addie. She may be cute as a button, but I guarantee she ain't worth all the hassle."

Yeah, right, I thought. *That's brilliant advice coming from someone who married a blonde bimbo he barely knew, one who's probably now going to take him for half of everything he has.*

"Where is she, anyway?" Gravel asked.

"She went on to bed. Said she'd had enough excitement for one day," I answered. "I don't think she's feeling her best today. Too much weed maybe."

"Ya know, you'd be better off keeping single and free," Gravel said.

"No offense, Gravel, but you're one to talk," I said.

"Yeah, well, learn from my experience, Trotter. Let 'em get too close and women just screw up your head and your life. Ain't never known one that didn't."

"Here's to women," I slurred. My neck was getting stiff, my eyes bleary, and I suddenly realized I hadn't eaten or slept in a long while. So I swallowed more of the smoothest vodka on earth, feeling it glide down my throat like a balm for the soul.

"But I guess that's their job – to bring us misery," Gravel continued. "Because it takes real misery t' make a real artist. We got way too much 'a that American Idol crap in the world. Singers, dancers, musicians…hell, they're all a dime a dozen. Ya got t' have balls and grit t' be a true star. Ya got t' be able t' reach down inside where all the dark shit lives, and pull the truth out, the pure, naked truth. 'Cause that's what people really want and all that really matters in the end. Somethin' that's real. Do ya know what I'm talkin' about, Trotter?"

61

For once, I truly did. At that moment, I understood Gravel Gold more than I ever had before or ever would again.

He rambled on, "Anybody can get some head shots, air brush a photo, take singin' lessons, pay somebody off, get on YouTube, or screw their way up into a better position. But that's all bullshit. Ain't none of it real."

Cows sauntered out in the morning sun to graze on an opposing hillside a hundred yards from where we sat. We watched them as though we'd never seen cows before.

"That's the life right there," I said. I was drunk.

"Betcha I could shoot one from here," Gravel said.

"Too far," I said.

"The hell it is." Gravel raised his pistol as if he might actually shoot.

"That's exactly what you need right now – to kill another beast of the field. A lion last night, a cow this morning," I said, and we both laughed till I thought we'd puke.

After the laughing fit subsided, I leaned back against the side of the house and tugged absently on my unkempt goat chin hair.

"I miss my mother," I said suddenly.

"Well, cry me a river," Gravel said sarcastically. "So why don't ya just go see her? Where is she?"

"She's dead. I've told you that before."

"Oh, yeah, that's right. Sorry."

"Don't worry about it," I muttered.

"Well, that was awkward," Gravel said, and paused for a long minute. "So, when did she pass?"

"Long time ago," I answered. "She had cancer when I was just a little kid."

The cows on the hillside had gathered around the watering hole as though they needed a drink after hearing the strange turn our conversation had taken.

Gravel slammed back a big gulp of whiskey and said, "Well, at least you had a mom for a while. At least she cared about ya, right? Mine was a sorry ass excuse for a mother. I hate her; always have and always will."

"Well, cry me a damn river," I said with a high-pitched voice, mocking him.

Gravel stared hard at me before busting out laughing. We both laughed so hard that we cried.

The cows took a vote and decided to eat some more grass.

After a little while, Gravel struggled to his feet and staggered inside. He came back out with two guitars. "Let's write a song," he said. And so we did. It was a drunken, weeping song of loss, anger and defiance. We wrote it on the patio and sang it to the cows.

My daddy was a drunk,
My momma skipped town;
They threw me in the swamp,
Hopin' to God I'd drown.
But I rose up on my two legs,
And I soared into the blue;
Now I don't need nobody,
And I sure as hell don't need you.
I shoot straight, straight from the heart,
And I don't give a damn
If it blows your world apart,
Cause I shoot straight,
Straight from my broken heart.

"Didn't get a chance to tell you," I said. "That was one hell of a party."

"Was, wasn't it?" Gravel said with a great, wide grin. "Betcha it'll be the main topic of conversation on Music Row come Monday mornin'."

"I suspect it will be the talk of a lot more than just Music Row."

I was right about that. All hell was about to break loose in Gravel's life. And mine.

The cows suddenly had company. There were a dozen reporters and photographers on the hillside, focused in on us with long range lenses. Two helicopters circled overhead and a crowd was gathering out front.

Gravel stood up and waved at the reporters on the hillside. Then he stepped inside and grabbed his shotgun. He pointed it skyward toward one of the low-flying helicopters. The chopper darted quickly up and away. "Damn right, you better get the hell outta' here," Gravel shouted.

"Come on, Trotter," he said. "Can't get no privacy nowhere these days. Let's go inside and screw some blondes."

"Uh, no, thanks. I'll pass," I said. "I'm worried about Addie. I'm gonna check on her."

"You did *see* the girls I got waitin' in there, right?" Gravel asked incredulously. "They are hot and ready as peach pies fresh outta the oven. And I got a feelin' it just might get a little rough and messy in the bedroom."

"I guess I'm just not in the mood for pie right now."

"Trotter, there's always room for pie."

13

Lions are people too.

The following morning, thousands of humans were gathered outside the security gate at Gravel Gold's mansion in Franklin to protest the death of one lion. They were fanning the flames of the firestorm that was suddenly threatening to consume the superstar's life. Every tabloid, animal rights group, and major news organization was represented in the chanting throng of humanity. The banners were many and varied: *Gravel Murders Helpless Creatures. Protect Animals FUR God's Sake. Thou Shalt Not Kill. Your Fur Had A Face. Gravel Kills – Love Heals. Jesus Was A Cat Lover.*

The Reverend Rutherford Loom was on television, making a statement regarding animal rights in general and Gravel Gold's brutality specifically. Mr. Loom was well-known as the pastor of the Wholly One World Church – the WOW Church, located in Hendersonville, Tennessee. He was also the founder and president of the newly formed animal rights organization called GLAT – God Loves Animals Too.

"The Lord God created every living thing and humans have no right to brutalize and slaughter God's creatures," Reverend Loom was saying to the crowd out front. A bemused Gravel Gold was watching the speech on television as it was being broadcast by a local news station.

The Reverend Loom continued, "This senseless death is a perfect example of the arrogance displayed by many humans toward the other living creatures with whom we share this planet. The killing of innocents must be brought to an end." A roar erupted from the crowd. Gravel, Addie and I heard the roar first as it emanated from the front of the house, then again as it came across the airwaves. Fueled by the mob's fury, the preacher rolled on.

"Some might say it's just a cat, just a beast of the field. Why should we care? My friends, we *must* care. The caring must start right here, today, now. Let it begin with justice for this beautiful creature that was cut down in its prime by one man's drunken foolishness. There must be retribution!" The crowd roared once again and began to chant, *Retribution. Retribution. Retribution.*

Fearing the demonstration might get out of hand, the authorities dispatched additional officers. A dozen police cars arrived on the scene with sirens wailing, and took defensive positions along the fence between the road and the mansion.

"Good God," Gravel said. "Are these people insane?" He turned to Addie and me and pleaded his case. "It was just a cat, a frickin' cat. And it was an accident. I didn't mean to kill the damn thing."

"You should tell them that," Addie suggested.

"Ah, those idiots ain't worth my time," Gravel snapped. "And their heads are so far up their asses that they wouldn't hear a thing I said anyway."

"You could at least try," Addie said.

"She's probably right," I said. "Might make you look a lot better to everybody in the long run."

"Since when have I ever cared about what people think? I don't play that game."

66

Gravel's phone buzzed. It was Cotton Black and Gravel took the call.

"Well, you really did it this time," Cotton said.

"Screw you," Gravel shot back. "Where have you been for the past eighteen hours while all this garbage was blowin' up? You're supposed to be my manager – you should'a been doin' some damage control."

"Some damage may be beyond control, my friend."

"Then what the hell are ya callin' for if ya ain't got any bright ideas or good news?"

The line was silent for a moment. "Tell you what," Cotton said. "How about Benji and I come out to the mansion so we can all talk about this situation? Let me think for a minute...should probably bring Spritzer, the PR guy from the label. He's pretty sharp. We'll sit down, just the four of us, think this thing through, hammer out our position and draft a press release. We'll hold a press conference and see if we can get public sentiment in your favor before things get any worse."

"Public sentiment," Gravel spit the words from his mouth with disgust. "I'll think about it and get back to ya."

"Gravel, you need to do more than thi--," Cotton tried to say, but Gravel ended the call.

"What a load of crap," Gravel mumbled.

Gravel's phone buzzed again. This time it was Gigi. She was brief and to the point. "I'll be living in the Malibu house now. I'm sending a couple of my girls to get some of my stuff from the mansion. You best keep your filthy hands off of them." Gigi paused and waited for a response from Gravel but got none.

"Divorce papers gonna be delivered tomorrow," she said.

"I'll be waitin' at the door," Gravel said.

Gigi was seething. "Sweetcakes," she said acidly. "I'm gonna make you wish you'd never met me."

"Honey pie," Gravel answered back. "You hit that mark in the first week."

"Go to hell," Gigi shouted and hung up.

Gravel tossed the phone on the counter and turned toward Addie and me. "Who's hungry?" he asked cheerily.

"We should call in a pizza," I laughed. "Can you imagine the delivery guy trying to get through the gate with that media circus out there?"

Gravel's phone buzzed again. "What is it now?" Gravel barked into the mouthpiece.

"Are you watching CNN?" Cotton said. "If not, you better turn it over there."

CNN had breaking news about a new Gravel Gold scandal. A young, blonde woman named Betsy Buffay was coming out to accuse Gravel of brutalizing her sexually. There were whispers that others would be coming forth with similar accusations as well.

"Hey, isn't that one of the three blondes from the party last night?" I asked.

Gravel moved close to the screen and peered in hard at it. "I'll be damned. I'd need to see her naked to know for sure, but I think that really *is* one a' them girls."

Ms. Buffay went on to describe her ordeal in considerable detail – how she was tied up with two other girls, verbally humiliated, emotionally scarred, and sexually violated by Gravel Gold with a microphone.

"You lyin' whore!" Gravel shouted at the screen. "You damn lyin' whore!"

Gravel got back on the phone with his manager. "Cotton, this is bullshit. I didn't do nothin' with them girls that they didn't want me to do. It's like the whole world's turnin' against me all of a sudden."

Cotton played the conversation diplomatically like a sly fox. He knew Gravel well enough – just as I did – to strongly suspect that there could be some truth to the woman's allegations. Cotton also knew that even more trouble was on the way – the label was planning to drop Gravel from their roster in a few days, and tie up his next record so that it would never be released to the public. Jimmy Bolen was exacting his revenge on the singer for having sex with his wife and publicly humiliating him.

Within the space of a week, Gravel could lose his record deal, lose his wife, lose at least half of what he possessed, face the firestorm of public outcry regarding the lion's death, and face legal challenges from women accusing him of sexual assault. It would be a tough week by anybody's standards.

14

Gigi, her posse, and her attorneys called from Hollywood a few days later. The video-conference was a sort of Come-to-Jesus meeting demanded by Gigi and arranged by her lead lawyer.

"I am suing your ass some more," Gigi said.

"More? What do you mean?" Gravel shouted.

"For libelations and slanderations against the defamation of my character."

Gravel grinned and rolled his eyes.

"I can *see* you," Gigi said.

"He stupid," Shonnaveesta said. "He too stupid for you." Shonnaveesta was Gigi's best friend; they'd met on the set of a music video a year earlier.

"I *know* you can see me, you stupid twat," Gravel said. "It's a video-conference call. I can see you too. Remember?"

Self-consciously, Gigi put a hand up to her hair, leaned toward the camera and whispered, "How do I look? Do I look okay?"

Shonnaveesta put a consoling arm around Gigi. "You look just fine, baby, just fine. You gorgeous. Any man be glad to have you." Then she leaned in close to the camera, her face filling our screen, and directed her remarks to Gravel. "And you better know, Mr. Gravel Gold, that you done let a good woman get away, and they's plenty of hot California men out here who's ready to scoop her booty up right now."

"Good riddance," Gravel said. "They can have her."

"Everybody in the world gonna hear your smart-ass attitude, Mr. Gravel Gold. Cuz this here goin' out on the world-wide web. Shonnaveesta gave a little wave, puckered her big lips up and blew a kiss into the camera. "And ya'll can come visit me at Shonnaveesta.com and follow me on Twitter at Shonna underscore Vista BBW."

"Just get the hell off camera, you stupid bitch," Gravel yelled. "Let me talk to my wife."

Gigi pushed back into the picture. "I ain't your wife anymore, you cheating bastard!"

"You're still my wife. We ain't divorced yet."

"Well, we're about to be. You cheated on me, you killed my kitty cat, and you defamed my character. Now I'm gonna take all your shit away from you."

"You just try, bitch," Gravel roared. "When I'm through with you, everybody's gonna see you for the garbage you really are. You married up and now it's time you go back down to the trailer park trash heap."

Shonnaveesta leaned back into the picture. "Ah, he think his shit don't stink. He think his shit come out gold. He got 'a lot to learn, baby."

"I told you to get off the camera," Gravel said.

"Oh, we gonna tweet you up, Mr. Gold. Gigi Nation gonna tweet you out the ass."

Gravel turned toward me and pleaded, "Can anybody tell me what she's talkin' about? What's this twitter and tweet crap?"

I shook my head and sighed. "Gravel, it's an online social media thing where people--"

"He don't even know about Twitter!" Shonnaveesta barked. "Like I said, he stupid."

Gravel pulled a pistol from a drawer and calmly blew the screen to pieces. He placed the smoking gun back

71

into the drawer and drawled, "Meeting adjourned."

15

The next morning, Gravel's phone rang. Seeing it was his manager, Cotton Black, he answered and grumbled a response before drifting back to dreamland with the phone on his pillow. The next thing he heard was Cotton shouting, "Come on, Gravel, wake up! This is important. You've got to trust me...doing this interview would be a good thing. You *need* to do this interview."

Gravel put the phone on speaker and rubbed the sleep and hangover from his eyes. "Good lord, Cotton, what are ya yellin' about?"

"I told you...I set up an exclusive interview for you with Dolly Richards at MMT. She is totally--"

"No, I don't wanna do no damn interviews," Gravel barked. "You know that."

"Yes, I know, but you need to be smart about this because you're running out of time. Dolly has always been a big fan of yours and she's sympathetic to your situation. She's willing to give you the chance to tell your side of things."

Gravel was silent.

"Are you still there?" Cotton asked.

"I'm thinkin' on it. Ain't Dolly that hot, good-lookin' redhead on MMT? Looks a little like Reba?"

"Yeah, that's the one. Any chance you could go up to the station this afternoon and talk to her? She's ready to move on this whenever you say the word."

"Alright, what the hell, I'll do it," Gravel said. "Tell her I'll be there at 2:00. I need to get out of the house."

"Yes, you do. And this interview is a smart move for you. Just keep yourself under control, be a nice guy, and tell your side of the story."

"Yeah, yeah, yeah, I know," Gravel grumbled. "Watch my language, play nice and don't offend anybody."

"Exactly," Cotton said. "I'll meet you there at two."

At 2:15, Gravel and Benjamin Wallows arrived via limousine at the downtown Nashville studios of MMT, Major Music Television. Gravel strolled in like the king of the world, wearing black from head to toe in honor of Johnny Cash, shades like his buddy, Bono, and a red bandana around his neck in honor of his old friend, Willie Nelson.

"You're late," Cotton said.

"Well, now, that ain't no way to greet your biggest client and your favorite cash cow," Gravel said with a smile as big as the rear end of a Clydesdale. "I bet you done hurt Benji's feelings."

Benjamin smiled weakly and said, "Hello, Mr. Black. I prepped Mr. Gold on the drive up and I think he's as ready as possible for this interview, considering the lack of advance notice. I believe we'd really be better off to reschedule for--"

"Oh, I'm sure he's as ready as he'll ever be," Cotton said, cutting Benji off.

"Hello, Mr. Gold," Dolly Richards said, extending her hand.

Gravel grabbed it and kissed it. "My, you sure do look lovely today, Ms. Richards."

"Thank you," Dolly said, withdrawing her hand carefully from his. "I appreciate you coming in for this interview."

"The pleasure's all mine, honeypot," Gravel said. "I watch your show all the time and I'm your biggest fan."

After a few minutes of makeup and readying the set, the program went live on the air with a special *Breaking Entertainment News* segment. As the introductory theme music played, Gravel leaned toward Cotton, who was just off-camera, and said, "Nobody said nothin' about this bein' live."

"Just roll with it, Gravel," Cotton said. "You'll be fine."

"I don't like this," Benjamin whispered, looking askance at Cotton. "I don't like this one little bit."

"Welcome to our special broadcast," Dolly Richards began. "Today we have with us in studio one of the world's most famous, yet most troubled superstars, Mr. Gravel Gold. With his career crumbling around him, he has agreed to speak with us today to tell his side of the story, to give us insight into the horrific events in which he has allegedly been involved."

Gravel's face grew stern and his jaw tightened as he listened to the host's opening statement. He flashed a very angry, dirty look at his manager, but Cotton did not make eye contact with him.

"Mr. Gold," Dolly continued. "You've been beset recently by such a staggering series of mistakes and bad publicity. How are you able to hold up under such a heavy load?"

Gravel gave the woman an icy stare that could have chilled the Devil. Through clenched teeth he answered, "I'm holding up just fine. What would make ya think I wasn't?"

"Well, I'm just assuming that the average person would likely be quite distraught in similar circumstances."

"Well, I'm not your average person, now am I?"

"Oh, most definitely not," Dolly said, with a glance into the camera and a slight, mocking raise of her right eyebrow.

"I thought I was here to tell my side of the story," Gravel said.

"Oh, yes, of course. Please tell us about your affair with Jazz Bolen, who is, of course, the wife of Jimmy Bolen, the president of your record label. As I understand it, one of the many sexual encounters between you and Mrs. Bolen was captured on video and broadcast to several hundred people at your residence. Can you tell us about that?"

Gravel shifted uncomfortably in his seat and sucked in an angry breath. He was fighting to maintain his composure, hoping that the long-term benefits of this interview might outweigh his temporary discomfort. Gravel wanted to respond with, *Yeah, it was some damn good, quality programming too...better than most of the slop that you put out.* But instead, he showed restraint and answered diplomatically, "My fans understand that I'm just a man, just regular folks like them. All of us are prone to make mistakes. Didn't you ever make any mistakes in your life, Dolly?"

"Well, I've made my share but I didn't broadcast them on television," Dolly said. "And I've certainly never sexually abused anyone, or punched a sickly, defenseless woman."

On the sidelines, Benjamin was enraged, and Gravel seemed as though he might shoot out of his chair and punch his interrogator. Instead, he said, "We should stick to one subject at a time, don't ya think?"

"Just a moment, please," Dolly interjected. "I'm getting word that we have been able to link up with another special guest today."

76

Puzzled, Gravel looked toward Cotton Black and said, "What's goin' on?"

Cotton shrugged his shoulders and mouthed, "I don't know."

Benjamin shed his normally unruffled demeanor and got in Cotton's face. "She's ambushed him, hasn't she? I thought she intended to be fair-minded."

Cotton smiled. "She's all about ratings and making a big splash."

"You...you set him up for this, didn't you?"

Before Cotton could reply, Dolly Richards swiveled toward the big video screen to her left, and began, "Ladies and gentlemen, we are now going to be joined by Gigi Gold, live from Los Angeles." Gigi's face appeared on screen. She was wearing far too much bright, red lipstick, sporting a childish splash of glitter on her cheeks, and her thick, blonde hair was piled up high and wild on her head.

"Welcome, Gigi," Dolly said. "Thank you so much for joining us. We're excited to get your input on all of this."

"I am just, like, so excited to be on here with you, Dolly. I just love your show. Shonnaveesta and I DVR all the episodes, and sometimes we have pajama parties, and stay up, like, all night long, drinking margaritas with the salt on the glass...you know the kind I mean? You ever have one of those? They are *so* good. And we sit up all night and watch you interviewing all the big stars. You are just, like, probably the best interviewer person of all time."

Gravel sat in stunned silence. The scene was so surreal, so absurd that it actually short-circuited his anger for a few moments.

"Well, that's quite a compliment, Gigi. Thank you very much," Dolly said. "I'm just curious though – who is Shonnaveesta?"

"She's my bestie," Gigi said. "My best friend in the whole world. Shonnaveesta been the one helpin' me through all this sadness since Gravel done broken my heart. Come here, girlfriend."

Shonnaveesta leaned into the picture. "Hi, I'm Shonnaveesta. I'm gon' be a superstar, so I go by that one name, jus' like them two old stars Madonna and Elvis are doin'. I want all the people out there to look me up at www dot shonnaveesta dot com. And I'm on Twitter too…my handle is–"

"Yes, yes, okay," Dolly interrupted. "Thank you for supporting Gigi through this difficult time."

Gravel cleared his throat loudly.

"Mr. Gold, would you like to address--" Dolly began

Gravel cut her off. "First of all, Vonnasheester, or whatever the hell your name is, you are a brainless idiot. Elvis had a last name and he used it – Presley. Second of all, he's dead now."

Incredulous, Dolly said, "That's your response to all of this? You want to quibble about a singer's name?"

"He's always like that. He thinks he's better than everyone else," Gigi shouted. "But I'm gonna take him down a few pegs and show him he can't keep taking advantage of women."

"You know, you didn't have a damn thing before I met you," Gravel said. "You were just another average blonde bimbo singin' at the bars when I found you."

"See how he, like, degrades women and stuff?" Gigi said. "What woman would want to live with that?"

"It's abuse, is what it is," Shonnaveesta chimed in once more. "Verbular abuse. He think he can get by with it, but not this time, mister. Gigi got you by the balls."

As the scene unfolded, Dolly Richards heard the voice of her producer whisper in her earpiece, "Jackpot. This is better than Springer's wildest dreams."

But Gravel Gold had had enough. He pulled off his microphone and threw it across the set, then kicked over his chair. "You can all go to hell," he shouted as he stormed off the set with Benji following close behind.

Outside the studio, a raucous crowd was waiting. They surged toward Gravel as he exited the building and headed toward the limo. Several reporters were close on Gravel's heels, shouting questions, "Mr. Gold, is it true that you punched a mentally ill woman in Pennsylvania? Why did you televise your sexual encounter with Jazz Bolen? Do you hate all animals or just cats? Did you rape Betsy Buffay with a microphone?"

CNN, Fox, and every Nashville station was live on the scene as Gravel gave them a double one-finger salute, jumped in his limousine, and sped away.

16

Gravel Gold was fighting hopeless battles on every front and he was losing the war. Gigi filed for divorce on grounds of adultery, and her case was obviously open and shut. She would chop off half of Gravel's kingdom in one quick blow. Animal rights groups were attacking Gravel via every available media outlet, and, like Michael Vick before him, Gravel was being slaughtered in the court of public opinion for animal cruelty. Betsy Buffay and the Pennsylvania woman were suing the superstar for abuse, and Gravel's attorneys were attempting to settle those cases out of court. Only a very large sum of money could make the whole ugly mess go away, and even that would never remove the stain and stigma that would be attached to the name Gravel Gold. As if all this wasn't enough for one man to bear, GMI tied up Gravel's new record in an interminable music limbo, with Jimmy Bolen vowing that the disc would never see the light of day. And finally, as one last slap in the face, the label was dropping Gravel Gold from their roster.

Jimmy Bolen and Gravel were standing on opposite sides of the GMI main conference room, separated by a thirty-foot long table made of African mahogany with a Purpleheart inlay of the GMI logo. Cotton Black sat in a plush chair near the middle of the massive table.

"Okay, so I banged your wife," Gravel said. "I confess. Ya got me. But we're both men here, and we both know shit happens. But what's done is done, right?"

The label president did not reply. He stood almost stone-faced, with only the slightest touch of an upward curl to the corner of his mouth, barely hinting at a smile. He seemed to be enjoying every second of the scene as it played out.

"Good God, you guys are actin' like it was frickin' Armageddon," Gravel said. "We're only talkin' about a woman here."

"Gravel, you really crossed the line this time, my friend," Cotton said. "I've been warning you for a long time to rein yourself in a little bit, to get a grip. But you just keep pulling stupid stunts like this."

"Come on, Cotton," Gravel said. "It was just a little sex. Didn't mean a thing."

"Do you know what makes it even worse, Gravel? You haven't even apologized one time," Jimmy said. "You had sex with my wife, publicly humiliated me, and never even bothered to say you were sorry."

"That's it? That's what you want? An apology? Hell, I apologize. I'm sorry I banged your wife. Now, can we just move on? Come on, whatta ya say?" Gravel stretched his arms out before him, hands up in a gesture of conciliation.

"What do I say? I say screw you," Jimmy said. "And screw your new record too."

Gravel turned on Cotton, pointing his finger. "You never should have let it come t' this."

"How is this *my* fault?" Cotton asked incredulously.

"You've been in Bolen's ear all along," Gravel said. "You been raggin' on my new projects, talkin' trash about it the whole time. You're my goddamn manager; it's your job t' see that things work the way they're supposed t' work. After all our years together, you're supposed t' believe in me and back me up all the way."

"You can't put this mess on me, Gravel," Cotton argued. "No way. You brought all this on yourself."

Gravel rubbed his thick, calloused hand over his face, scratching the ragged stubble on his jaw while he thought hard about the situation. Finally, he said, "Okay, if that's how you feel, then, you're fired."

"You can't fire me, you dumbass," Cotton said.

"The hell I can't," Gravel said. "You work for me and I can fire you anytime I feel like it."

"Not according to the agreement you signed."

"What the hell ya talkin' about?"

"The agreement you signed specifically states that my services on your deal can only be terminated by the label," Cotton said with a shit-eating grin.

Gravel looked from Cotton to Jimmy. "Is that true, Jimmy?"

"I'm afraid it is," Jimmy answered. He tossed a thick document on the table. "There, read it for yourself, like you should have done to start with. You'll find your signature on it."

Gravel straightened his back and pushed his chin out with a blend of defiance and resignation. "And you've both known about this all along."

Neither man responded. Gravel nodded his head slowly and said, "I see. I see how it is."

With lightning quick speed, Gravel leapt toward Cotton, grabbed him up by his shirt collar, and pulled his manager's face close to his. "You'll never screw me over again," he seethed through clenched teeth. "I promise you that."

"Come on, now, Gravel. Let go of Mr. Black. Why, there's no need for violence. Let's talk this thing out." Jimmy Bolen's tone was condescending and there was an evil lizard smile on his face.

Gravel glared like the noonday sun off the blade of a buzz saw.

"Listen to him, Gravel," Cotton stammered, struggling to breathe with his shirt pulled tight around his neck. "Don't do something else you'll regret."

"I already did. The day I signed up with you. And the day I signed that damn contract. Both of ya been screwin' me over since day one."

"I told you to let go of me," Cotton demanded, losing patience quickly.

Gravel snarled in Cotton's face like some kind of crazed animal. "I could hit you so hard you'd forget how to piss."

Cotton tried to pull free from Gravel's grip, but when that failed he foolishly punched the singer in the gut out of desperation. Gravel smiled for about a half second and said, "Ah, now, you shouldn't have done that. A man's got to defend himself when somebody slugs him." Gravel then delivered one quick blow to Cotton's face, busting his nose and lip, and sending him spiraling backwards into the plush, high-back executive chair.

"This relationship is over," Gravel said. "I'm done with the both of ya." He turned and left the room.

"You're done, alright," Jimmy Bolen said softly as the door closed behind Gravel. "You are toast."

17

"I miss those days when it was just about the music," Gravel mused, staring into his glass like he was a ten thousand miles away. "That's what I miss more than anything else."

I studied Gravel's face. It told a story of late night whiskey, early morning beer, unfiltered Camels, and a man who made it a habit to be always the headlights and never the deer. Weary lines of age, stress and hard living were showing themselves, the creases creeping slowly, inexorably across his dark, leathered Cajun skin. He looked like he'd aged twenty years in a week, and I felt sorry for the man.

"Yeah, I know how you feel," I said, for lack of anything better to say. I desperately wanted to find words of wisdom, something profound to share with him, but I had nothing.

"I've done a lot of stupid things in my life, haven't I?" he continued. "I remember my daddy used to say that I was dumb as a clump of dirt. Probably 'bout the nicest thing he ever said to me." He laughed dryly.

"Come on, Gravel, don't let this mess get the best of you. It's a tough situation but you can get through it. If anybody can, you can."

"Maybe I don't want to."

"What do you mean by that?"

Gravel waved a hand dismissively in my direction. "Aahhh, never mind. I'm just sick of all this crap, sick of Nashville, sick of people…fed up with the whole damn thing."

"That's understandable," I nodded. "Maybe you should just take a step back, you know, get away from it all for a while."

"Yeah, maybe," Gravel said. "I got this burnin' to make some real music again, make it like I did in the early days. Not this pathetic, stinkin' garbage that the record labels are always churnin' out now."

There was a long silence between us. Finally I asked, "So, what are you going to do?"

"Not sure yet. I'm studyin' on it, studyin' real hard. But whatever it is, you can bet it'll make one hell of a splash, like a meteor hittin' Lake Pontchartrain."

And with that, Gravel picked up his bottle of Jim Beam and went to bed. From the hallway, I heard him mumble, "Good night, Trotter."

It was the last thing he'd say to me for a long time, because the next morning, he was gone.

Part Two

18

It was a ranch-style farm house with a long, front porch, and it sat all alone on thirty acres of west Texas clay and loam in a clearing between two low-rolling ridges. Fifty miles west of San Angelo, the old home was situated at the end of a dirt trail that wandered aimlessly for ten miles before finding the nearest neighbor, and another ten before eventually meeting State Highway 163. The house had once been painted blue, decades ago, but now it was a dreary blend of weather-beaten grey and sun-baked brown.

The Middle Concho River ran through the property on its way from the Centralia Draw to the Twin Buttes Reservoir. Live oaks, mesquite and sagebrush dotted the landscape where bobwhite quail, blackbuck antelope, and turkey roamed free. It was a rugged and unforgiving land that the Comanche and Apache once ruled in the early 1800's. The small, widely-scattered hamlets in the region were ripe with back-country ghost stories and tales of knife-wielding phantoms in blood-stained clothing, and men with bears' heads who stalked the jagged ravines.

It was exactly the sort of place where one might go to disappear.

The old house had been built by Gravel Gold's great-great uncle in 1938, and he lived there until he passed away in 1967. After his death, the house remained in the family, abandoned and largely forgotten. Long before

Gravel's empire began to crumble, he'd secretly visited the old place and fell in love with its rugged isolation. He determined there and then that, with proper renovations, the house might one day make an excellent getaway or hideaway, should the need ever arise, and would also be a cool place to record an album.

Gravel prepared a list of necessary items, and instructed his ever-faithful assistant, Benjamin Wallows, to purchase them and have them delivered to the house by truck and helicopter. The entire project was handled in a clandestine manner, so that no one else, *absolutely no one* was aware of the covert operation. The truck driver and chopper pilot – both hand-picked by Benjamin – were sworn to secrecy and paid handsomely to remain silent.

Gravel's foresight had paid off. He was now living like a hermit, far off the beaten path, in his great-great uncle's well-stocked, little house on the prairie. The media was seeking him but could not find him. They wanted statements from him, interviews with him, and pictures they could splash all over the tabloids and magazine covers, but Gravel Gold had had enough. After ten years in the spotlight and the public eye, mired in the media mania, Gravel was relishing the temporary privacy and anonymity he found in his sagebrush seclusion. He was bitter and vengeful toward Gigi, Jimmy Bolen, the media, and the world in general, but this time, rather than lashing out, he was internalizing his rage. But only for a time.

Gravel's bruised ego and relentless hunger for the spotlight would eventually push him to emerge from the shadows, drive him back to center stage, and the process was well underway. He was drinking even more excessively than he ever had before, popping pills, smoking weed, writing, and recording around the clock, caught up in a gruesomely powerful fit of manic creativity. Gravel planned to make an epic explosion back into the entertainment headlines.

He had everything he needed for the recording project set up in his hideaway house, and was building a new record from the ground up, working feverishly because he knew that – even with his extremely covert operation – it was only a matter of time before someone discovered where he was. He had put down a thousand layers of drum, guitar, mandolin, keyboard, and vocal tracks; and by the time he was finished, would spend untold hours weeding through them, overdubbing and mixing. The record would be like nothing the world had ever heard before. He was certain of it.

And that's when the woman showed up.

Gravel was standing on the front porch sipping bourbon and smoking a cigarette, taking a brief break from the recording process. A figure appeared about two hundred yards away as it came up over a rise, walking briskly toward him. Gravel squinted and peered into the morning haze, trying to ascertain who was approaching and whether they might be a danger. He stepped inside, grabbed his 9mm, and slipped it in his back pocket just in case. Leaning against a porch post, he watched and waited. As the person grew nearer, he could see that it was a woman and that she was staring resolutely at him. She did not hesitate, but kept coming straight on until she reached the house. She stopped about ten feet from the porch.

"Good morning," she said firmly.

"You lost?" Gravel said.

"I am not lost," the woman replied. "Are you?"

Gravel grinned. He instantly liked her style.

The woman was petite and wiry, with black hair that was long and straight. She had dark skin, brown eyes, and high cheekbones. Gravel took her to be at least part, if not full, Native American. Her clothing was simple – blue jeans, tennis shoes, a white tee shirt, and a brown

91

leather jacket with fringes. She was pretty in a simple, earthy manner, not a classic beauty, and certainly not the Hollywood bombshell-type that Gravel Gold was more familiar with and typically attracted to.

"What's your name?" Gravel asked.

"Mackenzie," the woman answered.

"That your last name?"

"Mackenzie," she repeated. "You may call me Mackenzie. What may I call you?"

"You may call me Henry," Gravel answered with a smile, gently mocking her unusual diction and accent. He was instantly intrigued by the woman, and though he couldn't quite understand why, there was something strangely appealing about her.

"Are you making fun of me?" Mackenzie asked.

"Hell, no," Gravel said with a grin. "Never in a million years."

"May I have some water, please," Mackenzie asked. "I am very thirsty. I have had no water in a day."

"Sure, sure thing," Gravel said. "Come on in and have a seat." He quickly gave the woman two bottles of water and asked, "Where ya from?"

"West of here, about thirty miles, nowhere, really…a very small town, about fifty people," Mackenzie said.

"They're all small out here," Gravel said. "And very few and far between."

Mackenzie drank the water slowly, savoring it.

"How'd ya get here?" Gravel asked.

"I walked."

"You walked? Thirty miles?"

"Most of it. I caught a ride with a rancher for part of the way by horseback."

Gravel leaned back against the wall and tried to size her up. "You in trouble or somethin'?"

The woman held her head high and smiled. "Not anymore," she said.

Gravel wondered what that meant, but figured he'd let it alone for now, leave some mystery for later. "I bet you're pretty damn hungry," he said. "Ya want somethin' to eat?"

Mackenzie glanced around the filthy house stacked with garbage bags, cardboard boxes, cigarette butts, beer cans, weed buds, and liquor bottles. "Do you have anything edible here?" she asked doubtfully.

Gravel snorted and tossed a box of saltine crackers on the table. Surprised, she stared at it for a moment, then said, "Thank you."

Gravel sensed her disappointment. "Hell, I got plenty of other food around here. Most of it's frozen though. I just don't ever make much time for it."

"Perhaps I may look around your kitchen," Mackenzie suggested.

"Knock yourself out. My casa your casa and all that shit."

Mackenzie looked in the refrigerator, the pantry and all the kitchen cabinets. "You have everything you need. You could be eating well."

"Yeah, well, like I said…" his voice trailed.

"I will prepare something for us," Mackenzie announced. "I am an excellent cook."

Gravel sat in a chair with an acoustic guitar and played softly as Mackenzie cooked. He sipped his bourbon and watched her move about the kitchen as though she'd been born to the task. Her calm was mesmerizing. She hummed as she worked, ignoring him for the most part, only glancing his way occasionally and giving him a polite smile. Soon the disheveled house was filled with the pleasant aromas of sizzling pork chops, pinto beans, and fried potatoes. Gravel's stomach roared in response.

"Aint' ya the least bit nervous?" Gravel asked.

"About what?" Mackenzie said.

"About bein' out here in the middle of freakin' nowhere with a man ya just met."

Mackenzie's back was to him, and she replied simply, "My instincts tell me I can trust you. I don't believe you would try to harm me."

She slid a pone of cornbread into the oven and turned toward Gravel with a butcher knife in her hand. "Besides," she said. "If you try anything, I will slice off your testicles."

Gravel tipped his seat back and roared with laughter.

19

For the first three days, Addie and I didn't think much about Gravel's disappearance. Even in the best of times he was a wild card given to erratic behavior, willing to do anything on a whim. He was definitely not the sort of person who felt compelled to check in or answer to anyone; far from it. He always had a wide variety of projects and activities underway that he didn't tell anyone about, and he was prone to simply disappear from time to time. And even though I was one of his closest companions, there was still plenty I didn't know about him.

Our phones rang constantly. Friends, fans, musicians, business associates, attorneys, reporters, journalists, talk show hosts, and producers called daily. Tons of mail – both electronic and the old-fashioned type – poured in. Some of it came from diehard fans expressing their undying love and support for their idol, but much of it was hate mail. Animal lovers and champions of women's rights were especially vitriolic in their condemnation of Gravel Gold.

I did become increasingly concerned as the days turned to weeks, and I learned that Gravel had failed to show up for several important music-related meetings and court-mandated appearances. And when law enforcement officers came to visit, that's when I really got worried.

But I had no clue as to where Gravel was, and no one else seemed to know either – not his lawyers, Gigi, Cotton, Benji, the record label, Addie, or any of our band mates. Or at least, if they did, they weren't talking.

The media was in an uproar about the superstar's disappearance, and rumors were running wild. Some said he'd been kidnapped by Gigi's entourage, while others suggested he'd been abducted by aliens. There were even theories that he had been taken by the government to Area 51 or was hiding out with Elvis.

The hysteria mounted as hundreds of true Gravel Gold fans congregated daily in the areas surrounding the Gold mansion in Nashville, joining the hordes of animal rights protesters who'd already been there for two months. Not to be outdone, women's rights organizations were also camped out there, carrying signs and banners, giving speeches, and adding to the madness.

The media was all over it, of course. Every television talk show host and radio personality got endless play out of the entire mysterious affair, and it was constantly a top trending topic on Twitter. Of course, all of this led to increased sales of Gravel Gold music and merchandise, which in turn made the record label very happy. I surmised that they wouldn't keep Gravel's new record in cobwebs forever, as Bolen had threatened. The anger would cool eventually, and the greed would win out.

It was a hassle, to say the least, anytime Addie and I tried to leave the mansion. The crowds had to be herded out of the way, and then we had to be escorted out by armed guards. The police were there to help keep things under control, and someone – Gravel's attorneys, I supposed – called in extra private security to guard and protect the property and us. But it was still wearing on both of us.

"I can't take this anymore," Addie said, peeking out the window one day. "Look at them…they're driving me crazy."

"I know, I know," I said. "They need to get a life."

"Why won't they just go away? What do they think they're going to accomplish?"

"I wish I knew. I guess they feel like they've got to make their statement."

"Yeah, but how many times do they have to make it?" Addie asked, her voice rising. "Every day it's the same thing. I'm telling you, I just can't take this. Where the hell is Gravel? Why is he doing this?"

I shook my head slowly and said nothing.

Addie turned to me abruptly. "Do you swear to me that you don't know where he is? You wouldn't keep it from me if you knew, would you?"

I was very surprised by her question and attitude. "I told you I don't know. He just disappeared without saying a word."

"And you haven't talked to him since? Has he called you?"

I was getting pissed. "No, he hasn't called me. Why would I lie about it if he had?"

"You would if he told you not to tell anyone."

"I can't believe the way you're acting, Addie. Don't you trust me? If you don't like it here, you can always leave, you know."

"Maybe I will," she said defiantly. "I doubt we can stay here much longer anyway. It's not our house, you know. They're bound throw us out, probably sooner than later."

I said nothing more, but I knew she was right about that.

20

Nearly one thousand miles southwest of Nashville, far out in the deep, west Texas wilderness, Gravel Gold was adjusting to life with his unexpected houseguest. Though Mackenzie could be a bit annoying at times and had definitely interrupted his original plan, Gravel enjoyed her company for some reason he couldn't quite grasp. She was unlike any other women he'd ever known – both in appearance and attitude - and she carried herself with a calm strength and defiance. Most surprising of all, she didn't seem to care, or even know, who he was; and she was definitely not intimidated by him. And anytime she even hinted at the possibility of leaving, Gravel talked her into staying just a little bit longer.

Mackenzie was sitting up straight in her chair, hands folded in her lap. Gravel noticed that she never seemed to slouch. She was staring at him and it made him slightly uneasy. "So, you're a songwriter then," she said. "Will you sing one of your songs for me?"

"Sure," Gravel said. "Which one ya wanna hear?" Gravel was accustomed to his listeners knowing his full catalog and requesting songs by name.

"I don't know. Just something you wrote," Mackenzie said. "Play one of your personal favorites."

Gravel strapped on his guitar and stood in the center of the small room, surrounded by boxes, trash, and silence. He gazed down at his strange audience of one, and for the first time in years, he was nervous, actually nervous. The sensation startled him, shocked him, angered him. Mackenzie simply sat there, staring up at him with big, brown, innocent eyes, waiting for her song.

A wide range of emotions cascaded over Gravel and he clenched his teeth against the onslaught. He wanted to smash his guitar against the wall. He wanted to throw the woman out and forget about her. He wanted to go back to his mansion and live in luxury. He wanted to be in Central Park again, holding 1.2 million people in the palm of his hand, hearing them chant his name, hearing them worship him and only him.

"Don't be nervous," Mackenzie whispered.

He looked down at her, cleared his throat, and sang:

I'm sittin' here alone down in Music City,
Just me and my dreams, and it' ain't too pretty,
Cuz ten thousand others got the same dream.
Well, I sold the table where we used to eat dinner,
And sold the couch just to pay the rent,
Can't help but wonder, how much worse can it get?
And I pray to God, please get me through the night,
And I close my eyes and tell myself
It's gonna be alright.

Way off in the distance, I hear thunder,
And the sound of traffic out on I-24,
Can't help but wonder, what did I come here for?
Sometimes I laugh, sometimes I cry,
I sure do miss that look in your eye,
But most of all, I'm just tired of bein' alone.
And I pray to God, please get me through the night,
And I close my eyes and tell myself,
It's gonna be alright.
I pray to God it's gonna be alright

When he finished, Mackenzie's eyes were brimming with tears. "That's a beautiful, powerful song," she said. "You have a great gift. Your voice is…" her voice trailed off as she searched for the words she wanted. "So very soulful…mesmerizing…heart-wrenching," she said. "All of those things and more. I think you will be very successful if you pursue a career in music."

Gravel took off his guitar and said nothing.

"Please, play me another," Mackenzie said.

"Maybe some other time," Gravel murmured. He lit a cigarette, picked up his friend, Jim Beam, and they went walking among the sagebrush and cactus.

■ ■ ■ ■ ■

When Gravel returned, the house was filled with the luscious aromas of T-bone steaks, redskin potatoes, and black beans. It made him ravenous and he sat down at the kitchen table carefully. He'd drunk the entire fifth of bourbon while walking, more than enough to be drunk, but he wasn't. He was more shaken than drunk.

"If you keep cookin' like this, I'm gonna' be fat as a pig," he said. "That'll never work for my image. Hell, I ain't eat this much in years."

"My presence is disturbing you," Mackenzie said. "Do you want me to leave?"

"Do ya wanna leave?" Gravel asked back.

"Do you want me to leave?" Mackenzie repeated.

"Not if ya keep makin' steak like this. What'd ya do to it?"

"The secret is to cook it very slowly," Mackenzie answered. "I season it with garlic, black pepper, curry powder and other spices."

"Where'd ya find all that stuff? All them seasonings, I mean."

"Did you not know you have a box of spices in the cupboard?"

"Well, truth is, my assistant stocked the place with food and such."

Mackenzie looked skeptical. "Your assistant? Well, perhaps you could have your assistant bring some eggs, fresh milk, real butter--"

"Make a list," Gravel said.

"What?"

"Just write down whatever ya need and I'll see that ya get it. Might be a few weeks, but you'll get it."

"Alright, then," Mackenzie said slowly. "Thank you."

"Ya know, ya look a lot like a girl I used t' know," Gravel said, his mouth full of steak.

"Eat some potatoes and beans," Mackenzie said.

"I'm eatin' my damn steak."

"You drink too much alcohol," Mackenzie said. "Your body needs a variety of nutrients to repair the damage you are doing to yourself."

"Don't need nobody tellin' me how much alcohol to drink or how much food to eat. I been eatin' since I was a baby."

"Who was she?" Mackenzie asked, as she busied herself in the small kitchen, cleaning counters and dishes.

"Huh?"

"You said I remind you of a girl you knew."

"Oh, yeah," Gravel said, chewing his steak, wishing he hadn't said anything to begin with.

"What happened to her?" Mackenzie persisted.

"She's dead," Gravel answered.

"We all die," Mackenzie said.

Gravel raised his eyebrows, surprised by her cold remark.

"It's what we do before then that matters," she added.

Gravel nodded slowly and considered that.

"What do you do?" Mackenzie asked. "What do you do before you die?"

"I write songs," Gravel said.

"Why?"

"What the hell do you mean *Why?* You sure do ask a lot of stupid questions," Gravel said, shaking his head and stuffing more T-bone into his mouth.

"Why are you so afraid to answer questions? Perhaps it is the answers you fear more than the questions."

Gravel straightened in his chair and put both hands firmly on the table. "Look, lady, I just don't like bein' interrogated with a bunch of goddamn questions," he said angrily.

"You should be ashamed for taking the Creator's name in vain, and for all of the other horrible words you use so often. Can't you express yourself without constant profanity? A filthy mouth indicates a filthy mind and heart."

Gravel stood up abruptly and yelled, "What are ya, some kind of holier-than-thou missionary sent here to preach at me?"

"I am here because I have nowhere else to go," Mackenzie said softly.

Her statement hit Gravel like a brick in the gut, and he sat back down hard in his chair. "Me too," he said.

21

"Well, I guess we know why Gravel hasn't been answering his cell phones," I shouted as I rushed down the mansion's main staircase.

"Why? What is it?" Addie asked.

"I was going through Gravel's room just now, looking for anything that might give us a clue where he'd gone, and I found all his phones in a bag with a bunch of other stuff. It was stuck in the back of one of the closets."

"I bet he left them so he couldn't be tracked," Addie suggested. "They can trace your phone with radar and computers and stuff, right? I've seen it in movies."

"Not radar; GPS is how they do it," I said. "I'd say this means he really is hiding out somewhere, and doesn't want anyone to find him."

"Well, he can't hide forever, can he?" Addie asked.

"I don't think he'd even want to; that's just not his style. You know as well as I do that Gravel needs to be in the spotlight more than anything else."

The front door opened; it was Benjamin Wallows.

"Hi, Benji," Addie said, giving him a quick hug. "Haven't seen you much lately. How have you been?"

"Hello, Addie, Trotter. I have just been…well, there's so much going on lately," Benjamin said, somewhat nervously, before changing the subject. "Oh, my God, it is such a madhouse out there! All those people chanting and whatnot…it gets a little bit scary, doesn't it?"

"Yeah, and it's a real pain in the ass," I said.

"Have the two of you found a new place yet?"

"Uh, no, not yet," I answered slowly.

"We've talked about it...and looked a little bit," Addie offered.

"Is there a timetable on it?" I asked.

"Well, yes, I thought you knew," Benjamin said. "They're saying the house has to be empty by the first of the month."

"Wow, I didn't know that," I said. "I figured we'd have to move out, you know, eventually....but I didn't know they had set a date. We were just sorta watching to see how it all played out."

"Well, I'm sorry to be the bearer of bad news," Benjamin said.

Addie plopped down in a big plush chair and whined, "What are we going to do, Trotter? Where will we go? How will we ever find a place this cool?"

I rolled my eyes in Benjamin's direction. Sometimes Addie said or did things that reminded everyone of her immaturity. "Addie, we've basically been on borrowed time here. This is one of the finest mansions in the entire country, and we've been living here rent free. Believe me, we *won't* ever find a place or a deal like this again."

Addie crossed her arms and huffed a bit. "Well, what are they gonna do with it? Is Gigi gonna move back in? Maybe we could stay with her. I mean, she's not mad at us, right? We didn't do anything wrong."

Benjamin shrugged his shoulders. "I have no idea what's going to happen. The whole thing is such a huge mess. Attorneys are fighting it out over all the lawsuits and the divorce. Who knows, they may auction off the place."

Abruptly, I changed the subject and asked Benjamin a pointed question, "Tell me the truth, Benji. Do you have any idea where Gravel is?"

"No," he answered a little too quickly and sharply. "How should I know what's happened to him? He probably left the country."

I shook my head. "No, I can't imagine that, considering how Gravel likes to keep his feet planted on American soil as much as possible. Wouldn't seem likely that he'd run off and hide on another continent."

"Well, I'm sure I don't know. Your guess is as good as mine."

"Seems like he would have confided in *someone* about what he was doing. And you're his right hand man."

"Are you accusing me of covering up something?" Benjamin fired back. "You are his best friend and guitar player. Seems to me that if he'd confided in anyone, it would have been *you*."

I put my hands up in front of me in a gesture of conciliation. "Hey, I was just asking, Benji. Didn't mean to offend you."

"It's okay. I'm sorry," Benjamin said, as he gathered some papers from a file cabinet. "This whole thing just has me on edge."

Addie gave him another hug. "Don't worry, Benji. We know how much you love Gravel. We love him too. He'll show up soon."

Benjamin gave her a weak smile. "Thanks, Addie. Now, I am really sorry but I have to run. Good luck finding a new place."

I stared at the big, dark door for a very long minute after it closed behind him.

"What are you doing?" Addie asked.

"Something's up," I answered. "Did you see how he overreacted when I asked him about Gravel? He was really upset."

"He's probably just worried about him. And you know he has a super crush on Gravel, right?"

"Yeah, but it's not that."

105

"You really think he knows where Gravel is?"

"Maybe so. He definitely knows a lot more than he's telling," I said, still staring at the door.

"Hey, I almost forgot!" Addie said suddenly. "Have you heard the news about Gigi? She and Shonnaveesta started a singing group. I was just watching it on TV right when you found the phones."

"You have got to be kidding," I said. "Those two singing together? That's a scary thought."

We went online and got the full scoop. Gigi Gold and Shonnaveesta had teamed up to form a duo called 2VBW, which stood for two virgins, black and white. They'd already recorded and released their first single, "Pump It Hard." We clicked on the video, and I gaped at the screen, speechless.

"Oh, my God," Addie exclaimed. "It's so awesome."

I looked at her in disbelief. "What? Are you joking? This is an embarrassment to real music and artists everywhere."

"You're just saying that because you don't like Gigi."

"I *do* like Gigi," I argued. "But this song sucks. And look at her dancing...if you can call it that. She's terrible."

Addie paused for a moment and laughed. "Well, you're right, she really can't dance. But it doesn't matter because she's so weird and sexy. She really gets her freak on."

I couldn't help but think about what Gravel said to me the night before he disappeared, about missing the way music used to be. And watching Gigi Gold and Shonnaveesta do hackneyed dance moves to programmed drum tracks made me feel ancient. It reminded me once again of the fourteen year age difference between me and Addie. That gap seemed more like a chasm as I watched her bop around the room to the first release from 2VBW.

22

Gravel and Mackenzie had settled into a comfortable living arrangement as the weeks turned into months. Gravel worked day and night on his album, and the songs seemed to be taking a new direction, growing deeper, richer, and more vibrant. The powerful darkness remained in his music, but it was touched with a glimmer of hope.

Mackenzie busied herself on the house, and tried to give Gravel his space as much as possible. She made no complaints and no demands, simply set about cooking, cleaning, and organizing.

"I am a simple person," she said. "I do not ask for much."

"What *do* you ask for?" Gravel asked.

"I want only a place to dwell, food to satisfy my hunger, enough work to keep my hands busy...wisdom, honesty, love. These are the things I seek. What else is there?"

"What about money, jewelry, makeup, clothes and all the other crap that most women care about?" Gravel asked. "What about all the modern conveniences the world has t' offer? Fancy houses, fast cars, video games, plasma screens...are ya tellin' me ya don't give a damn about any of that?"

"That is exactly what I am telling you."

Gravel shook his head dubiously. "You're missin' out on a heck of a lot."

"I am from a tiny village on Indian land. I was raised by very strict parents, spiritual, you might say. They were devoted to the old ways, as our family has been for generations. In our home, we had no television or other modern entertainment devices. My father would not permit it. They taught me to seek higher things, to be more concerned with the inner matters of the heart than the outer trappings of modern society. As the Bible says, 'Where your treasure is, there will your heart be also'."

Mackenzie continued, "I married a man in our town I'd known since childhood. But the man I found inside the bonds of marriage was nothing like the man he had seemed to be from the outside. I was devoted to him but he was not to me. When I stood up to his wickedness and infidelity, he struck me in his anger and shame."

"And so ya left him," Gravel said.

"I left him. I am an intelligent woman, but I can be very impulsive."

"Yeah, I picked up on that right away," Gravel said. "So, what happened?"

"I traveled thirty miles and ended up here with you."

Gravel rubbed his big hand across his whiskers and said, "Son of a bitch. Hell of a story."

"What's done is done," Mackenzie said.

"And you really don't know who I am?" Gravel asked.

"I know exactly who you are, Henry," Mackenzie answered. "You're a lonely man in a farmhouse on the prairie."

Then she kissed him on the cheek and left the room.

Gravel put his elbows on the table and his head in his hands. He breathed deeply and exhaled, blowing the breath out hard, as if he could also push out the confusion that was swirling inside him.

108

"What the hell am I doin'?" he muttered to himself. "I was out here by myself, doin' just fine, makin' my damn record until this woman comes along...and now...and now what? I'm talkin' t' myself, that's what. She's screwin' with my brain."

He strummed through some chord progressions on his guitar, feeling them, finding them, letting them bounce off the walls and resonate in his soul. He knew the old familiar feeling as it came upon him, and he switched on the recording machine to tape the new song as it poured forth from his heart:

I lay me down beside you but I can't sleep,
All I can do is think and think and think,
Staring at your face, watching you breathe,
Hoping and praying that you'll never leave.

Had a long line of red tail lights
Backed up in my brain,
Eighteen-wheelers hauling loads of pain,
But that was before you came along,
And made sweet love to me all night long.
Now, even the angels...must be...
A little jealous...of me......tonight...

I used to think that I was so damn smart,
Talking the talk but running from my heart,
Now in your arms I finally understand,
That a little bit of love can heal a man.
Yeah, a little bit of love
Can heal a broken man.
And even the angels...are bound to be...
Just a little bit jealous...of me...
Even the angels...must be...
A little bit jealous...of me...tonight...

23

The helicopter blades sliced through the warm morning air over west Texas, and blew up a small dust storm as the chopper sat down near Gravel Gold's hideaway. Gravel was in his work room with headphones on, setting EQ levels and mixing tracks on his newest creation. Mackenzie grabbed a shotgun and pounded on Gravel's door, even though she'd been warned not to disturb him when he was recording.

"Henry! Henry! Someone is here!" she shouted at the door.

At a break point in the music, Gravel heard the pounding. Angrily, he shouted back, "I'm workin' in here. What the hell do ya want?"

"Someone is here," she repeated. "Come quickly." Mackenzie did not wait for him. She ran out onto the porch and pointed the shotgun at the intruders. "Stop right there," she shouted at the thin man as he approached the house. He was wearing khakis and a lime sweater vest over a neatly pressed dress shirt. "Stop and keep your hands where I can see them."

"Oh, crap," Gravel said, jumping up. "Wait up a minute, Mac!" He ran outside where his faithful assistant, Benjamin Wallows, stood trembling with his hands in the air, probably about to pee his pants.

Gravel took the weapon gingerly from Mackenzie. "Whoa, now, Mac. Calm down," he said. "This here's my assistant, Benji."

"I have asked you not to call me Mac," Mackenzie said. "And as for my behavior, I was simply defending our property from intruders."

"*Our* property?" Gravel chuckled.

"We live here together, do we not?" Mackenzie said.

Gravel took a deep breath and decided to drop the topic. He looked at Benjamin, forlorn in the Texas dust. "Benji, ya can put your arms down now," Gravel said.

"Who is this woman?" Benjamin asked.

Before Gravel could speak, Mackenzie stepped off the porch and grasped Benjamin's hand. "I am Mackenzie. I sincerely apologize for threatening you."

"Uh, well, alright, then," Benjamin said tentatively. "I suppose I can accept your apology." Then Benjamin turned to Gravel and quietly said, "Mr. Gold, may I speak with you for just a moment?" They walked a short distance away from the house, out into the brush and cacti.

"Who is this woman and where did she come from?" Benjamin asked with respectful concern. "I don't trust her...she could be a plant sent here to get a story and to reveal your location to the world."

Gravel laughed. "Benji boy, I appreciate your dedication to duty and for lookin' out for me, but she ain't no damn spy. She's just an Indian woman who came wandering through the desert one day. I know it sounds pretty weird but it's the truth."

Benjamin raised his eyebrows nearly up to his hairline and said, "I'm sorry, Mr. Gold, but that does sound terribly suspicious. Please allow me to investigate her background." Benjamin pulled out a small electronic notebook. "Do you know her full name?" he asked quietly.

111

"Mackenzie. That's all I know," Gravel said. "And you won't find nothin' 'bout her in any frickin' database, I guarantee it. Stop worryin', Benji boy. She don't know anything about the rest of the world. She don't even know who the hell I am."

"What? How can she not know who you are? That's ridiculous," Benjamin exclaimed with obvious umbrage.

"Come on, Benji, let it go. Relax." Gravel slung his arm around Benjamin's shoulder. "You seem a lot more tense than usual. Somethin' botherin' ya? Spit it out."

"Well, sir," Benjamin hesitated. "The search for you has intensified and some people think I know where you are. They interrogate me and some even accuse me of withholding information. Even Trotter questioned me about it. I feel like a criminal."

"Easy now, Benji," Gravel said. "Don't get your panties up around your ears."

"But I could get in a lot of trouble, couldn't I? And every time I come out here with supplies, I do my best to be secretive, to make sure that absolutely no one is following me or aware of my activities. That's why this trip was delayed so long. I'm afraid someone will eventually find out. It's really a lot of pressure, Mr. Gold, and I'm worried." There were tears in Benjamin's eyes.

Gravel put his hands gently on Benjamin's shoulders and spoke softly. "Whoa, now, listen here. First of all, I'll tell ya this much – it ain't gonna be much longer. The new record is almost done. And second of all, I give you my solemn word that I will not let you get in any trouble. You've been the only one I can really depend on and you've saved my ass more times than I can count over the years. Even when I'm dead and gone, you'll be well taken care of, Benjamin."

Benjamin Wallows was overcome with emotion; he dabbed at his eyes and grinned widely.

"What?" Gravel asked. "Why you lookin' at me like that?"

"You called me *Benjamin*."

Gravel smiled, mussed his assistant's hair, and joked, "Well, desperate times call for desperate measures." Then he turned and pointed back toward the helicopter. "Now, tell me, who's the chopper pilot? That's not Bubba."

"Sorry, Mr. Gold. It was necessary to use a different pilot," Benjamin answered. "Bubba was quite ill."

"You sure we can trust this guy?" Gravel asked.

"Oh, absolutely," Benjamin said, gazing at the pilot longingly. "His name is Charles, and he is my very dear friend." Charles was 6'4" with muscular arms, a shaved head, a strong jaw line and a trim, buff figure.

The way Benjamin said the words *very dear friend* made it clear to Gravel that the two were lovers. Gravel nodded and said, "Alright, Benji boy, if you vouch for him, he's alright with me. Have him unload the supplies and bring 'em on inside."

After the gear, food and other provisions were brought into the house, the four of them sat in the living room.

"Charles, do ya drink?" Gravel asked, offering up his bottle of Jim Beam just to see how Charles reacted.

"Yes, I most certainly do," Charles replied. He snatched the bottle quickly from Gravel's hand and took a long drink.

"Son of a bitch," Gravel exclaimed. "He's a keeper, Benji boy."

"Charles," Benjamin said, stretching his name out as a mother might when scolding a wayward child. "You shouldn't encourage him, Mr. Gold. He gets a little crazy when he drinks too much." Benjamin strongly emphasized the last three words of his sentence, and addressed them sharply at Charles.

"I got a little somethin' else, if you're interested, Charles," Gravel said as he retrieved a blunt from a box under the couch, and lit it. "This is some fine weed. They call it White Rhino."

Benjamin knew there was no use arguing with Gravel regarding mood-altering substances. He gazed around the room and said, "The house looks different...so much..."

"Cleaner," Mackenzie offered.

"Yes, that's it," Benjamin said. "The last time I was here bringing supplies to Mr. Gold, it was rather--"

"Filthy as a nasty pig's sty?" Mackenzie said.

"Yes, that's it, exactly," Benjamin said, nodding his head vigorously. He smiled warmly at Mackenzie. "I suppose we have you to thank for the improvement."

"She's a regular frickin' Martha Stewart," Gravel said.

"I do not like disorder. One's home is a reflection of one's soul," Mackenzie said, sitting up quite straight and proper in her chair, as was her custom.

Gravel and Charles drank Jim Beam while Benjamin attempted to interrogate Mackenzie without her being aware of it. After the shotgun greeting she'd given him, he should have known better. Gravel simply watched and smiled as he inhaled the best Brazilian cannabis money could buy.

"So, Mackenzie, I imagine it must have been very difficult for you to find your way here," Benjamin said. "How did you survive in that wasteland?"

Mackenzie answered matter-of-factly, "How does the eagle soar? How do the roots of the Juniper tree find water in the driest seasons?"

Benjamin did his best to maintain a nonplussed expression. "Well, I suppose they act according to their nature," he answered. "And so, I assume surviving the wilderness comes naturally to you." He switched casually to another subject, hoping to extract information from this unusual woman. "So, tell me, Mackenzie, do you listen to much music where you're from?"

"Certainly. Music has always been very important to me and my family."

Benjamin glanced subtly at Gravel with a hint of a smile, as if to say, *Aha!* "Do you have any favorite songs?" he asked.

"The song of life," Mackenzie answered.

"Um, I don't think I know that one," Benjamin said.

"Oh, certainly, you do," Mackenzie said. "Listen. Listen closely."

Benjamin looked puzzled. "Uh, what exactly am I listening for?"

"Do you hear the earth, the wind, your heart beating within you? The song of life, Benjamin...it courses through you, me, and all things."

Gravel roared with laughter. "Yeah, Benji, don't you recognize the song of life? My aunt had the forty-five and I used to listen to it when I was a kid. You hear it, don't ya, Charles? Ain't it beautiful?"

"As beautiful as a puckered pink butthole," Charles proclaimed with a silly grin.

Gravel and Charles were quickly reaching a state of joyful inebriation and happy high. Charles leaped to his feet and began to dance about the room. Gravel grabbed his guitar and ran through an assortment of vibrant chord progressions. Charles' white teeth sparkled in the sun beams that streamed through the window, and he sang with a glorious vibrato, making the song up as he went along:

The song of life...courses through you,
Toast the song of life...with a bottle of brew,
Up from the earth...and down with the rain,
This bud is the bomb...blowing up my brain.

Charles took Benjamin by the hand and tried to lift him up from his seat. "Dance with me, Benjamin, dance to the song of life with me," he pleaded. But Benjamin was far too shy to display such uninhibited behavior outside the privacy of his bedroom, and especially in the presence of Gravel Gold, his boss and the man he had long revered and adored.

"I apologize for Charles' behavior, Mr. Gold," Benjamin said. He then turned his attention to Charles and said, "We are here on business, conducting an important assignment, and you're embarrassing me in front of my employer."

"Benji...Benji boy, you need t' lighten up and enjoy yourself," Gravel said. "Ain't nothin' more entertainin' than a flamin' gay guy buzzed on bourbon and bud."

"That would be me!" Charles announced with an exaggerated cockney accent and a flamboyant pirouette.

"But, Mr. Gold, Charles is obviously in no condition to pilot the helicopter. We won't be able to leave until he sobers up."

"Not a problem. You'll just stay overnight and fly back tomorrow," Gravel said.

"Well, yes, I suppose we should do that since it's gotten so late," Benjamin said

"But the two of ya ain't sleepin' with me, I'll tell ya that right now. To each their own, but personally, I don't want no damn wiener up the butt in the middle of the night."

24

Gigi and Shonnaveesta rocketed to the top of the Pop charts with their first hit and became superstars within a matter of weeks. They made the rounds on all the late night talk shows and even some of the early ones, although neither woman was particularly fond of waking before noon. But like a carnival freak show on wheels, they traveled the country spreading their "music" and America ate it up. The duo was offensive, ignorant, and caused an uproar everywhere they went; and while critics hated them, the public couldn't get enough of 2VBW.

Gigi decided to drop her last name, Gold, and follow Shonnaveesta's lead in becoming a one-name celebrity. But every chance she got, Gigi didn't hesitate to remind everyone that, for the time being, she was still married to the man who *used to be* King of the Pop World. For as long as she could milk something out of it, she was using Gravel's name and money as a springboard to success. And wherever in the world Gravel was, Gigi secretly hoped that he was watching, and was doing her best to rub her success in his face.

But she had no way of knowing that Gravel was still secluded in the wilderness, intentionally cut off from all outside news and communication, other than the snippets of information Benjamin passed along on his very rare visits to bring supplies. Gravel had no television or online access – not that he'd ever had much interest in those things to begin with – and no way yet of knowing that his estranged wife and her new partner were conquering the entertainment world, and mocking him in the process.

The second single from 2VBW entitled "Girl Don't Need No Man" was the epitome of that mockery. It featured a big, goofy-looking man dressed in black who was an obvious parody of Gravel Gold. The video made him out to be a complete buffoon and an object of ridicule; and the repeated refrain in the song was "Girls don't need no man like that, that's right, girls don't need no man."

In addition to a growing list of other endorsement opportunities – hair care products targeted at teenagers, and a video game that pitted southern girls against zombies – Gigi also retained her role as the spokesperson for the Itty Bitty Cat Food Company. They, of course, had to get a new lion, and this time they selected a male named Hector to costar with Gigi in their commercials.

Without discussing it first with Shonnaveesta, Gigi decided to use Hector in the third video from 2VBW, a song entitled "Don't You Pet My Pussycat." When Shonnaveesta showed up at the video shoot, Hector was lounging in the middle of the room

"What the hell is that?" Shonnaveesta complained loudly, pointing her long gold fingernail at the big cat. "That a lion?"

Gigi half-pranced, half-clomped across the room excitedly atop her neon green, chunky, high-heel, lace-up platform boots, and screamed, "Oh, Shonna, ain't he beautiful? He's gonna be, like, starring in the video with us!"

Shonnaveesta put her hands on her hips, swung her head sharply from side to side, and said, "No, no, no, no, no, no."

118

Gigi gave out a high-pitched, ear-splitting whine, and cried, "But why, Shonna?"

"Shonnaveesta don't work with no animal what can eat her."

"But he's tame and trained, and he's so sweet. Just look at him…he wouldn't hurt a fly."

"Gigi, what part of 'no, no, no, no, no, no' do you not understand? Listen here, girl. I loves you bunches and you're my bestie, but you need to get it through your sweet, honky head – Shonnaveesta don't work with no damn lions."

"But I want Hector in the video," Gigi pouted.

Shonnaveesta began naming felines and counting off on her fingers, "No lions…no tigers…no lepers…no cheaters…no bobcats…no panthers…"

Robert Rain, the director of the music video, had years of experience in dealing with hard-to-handle musicians and singers, and he stepped in to calm the storm. "Ladies, relax. This is not a problem at all," he said. "Shonnaveesta, we can film your parts without the lion even being in the same room with you. Then we'll just put it all together in the editing process. We can solve everything through the wonders of modern technology. How does that sound to you?"

Shonnaveesta chewed on her lip. "Well, I guess that be okay."

"And what about you, Gigi?" Robert asked softly, as though he was speaking with a child. "Does that sound like a good plan?"

Gigi twisted her hair and said, "Sure, that's a good idea. I just wish Shonna would love Hector like I do."

On the other side of the room, the lion shook his mane and growled a little. It was the perfect example of bad timing.

Shonnaveesta raised her eyebrows at Gigi and said, "Oh, baby, that ain't gonna happen."

25

The wind was rushing across west Texas, bringing heavy rain and fearsome bolts of lightning. The old farmhouse had felt this wrath before and it shook beneath the onslaught but held its ground. Gravel Gold and Mackenzie were in the house alone, waiting out the storm, listening to the crack of thunder and the sound of limbs and debris blowing against the walls and roof.

Mackenzie sat up straight in her chair, peering into the flames dancing in the fireplace. "I remember a storm like this when I was a little girl," she said. "Lightning struck the tallest tree in our town and split it in half straight down the middle. One side of the tree was torn away, but the other remained and thrived. The bad side was scorched black and smoked for days, but the good side burst out in beautiful blooms the very next morning. It was a miracle from God."

Through bleary, blood-shot eyes, Gravel drank his bourbon and watched Mackenzie as she spoke, mesmerized by her, gazing upon her as if in a trance.

"The tree had healing power after that, and everyone spoke of it with great awe," Mackenzie continued. "Those with illness or injury could touch the good side and be healed. My parents took me to the tree when I burned my hand in a fire just like this one."

She held up her hand and rotated it slowly for Gravel to see. "I was in much pain and my skin was blistered badly. My father took me to the tree and spoke to the spirits, and my hand was healed immediately."

Mackenzie looked at Gravel and asked, "Do you believe in such things?"

"I'm a Cajun. Seen and done enough voodoo in my time to know anything's possible," Gravel said. "But most time I don't run my life by magic or miracles or faith. I just do what's got to be done. Nothin' was ever give to me the easy way. When I wanted something, I took it, and if anybody got in my way, I grinded their ass down in the dirt. I'll tell ya this much, Mac, I don't care what Jesus said - the meek ain't gonna inherit the earth."

"That is very sad," Mackenzie.

"Maybe, but that's just the way things are. I tell it like it is."

"Why must you drink so much?" Mackenzie asked, watching him finish off the bottle and go for another. "You are killing yourself with alcohol."

Gravel grinned at her and said, "Well, ya said it yourself, Mac…we all got to die."

"Perhaps you might try surrounding yourself with friends and loved ones rather than wrapping yourself up in liquor."

"Let me tell you somethin' 'bout people," Gravel said, swaying just a bit in the middle of the room under the influence of Jim Beam. "Ya can't trust 'em but only a little bit, because they're bound to let ya down. They *always* let ya down."

Gravel turned and spit a mouthful of bourbon into the fire for fun, just to watch it flare up.

Mackenzie was having none of his bitter story. She said, "You drink too much, smoke too much, curse too much--"

Gravel cut her off, "And you talk too much."

There was a knock at the front door, weak and uncertain, barely audible above the roar of the storm, but a knock nonetheless.

Gravel laughed loudly. "You expectin' company, Mac? Good God, I come to the wilderness to get away, and it's like a freakin' Grand Central Station out here."

Gravel grabbed his .357 and pulled the door open with a roar. A small, frail man fell into the living room floor. He was an old Indian with long, silver hair, and he wore blue denim clothing, moccasins, and a cowboy hat. Soaked to the bone, muddy, and weak, his stomach was empty but his eyes full of visions.

Gravel and Mackenzie laid him on the couch and covered him with blankets. Mackenzie brought him hot tea and sat beside him, comforting him, trying to coax him to drink.

"I am a code talker," the Indian mumbled.

"What does that mean?" Mackenzie asked.

"In the Great War, I directed the forces of the nation against the Japs," he said weakly.

Mackenzie looked at Gravel who shrugged. "Poor old guy sounds delusional to me."

"Here, drink this," Mackenzie said, lifting his head gently and putting the cup to his mouth. "Tell me, what kind of code did you use?" she asked, hoping to humor and soothe the old man.

The Indian looked surprised and pursed his lips, wondering how such a foolish question could be asked. "We used the native tongue, of course. We guided our soldiers and crushed the Japanese armies...and they never, *never* broke our code. *Diné bizaad yee atah naayéé' yik'eh deesdlíí'. Beh na ali tsosie* was for slant eye. Dive bomber was *gini* which means chicken hawk. *Besh lo* means iron fish...that was submarine."

"So, you were a soldier?" Mackenzie asked.

"In the heat of battle, with lives at stake, we made no errors in our codes. They trusted us. Not at first, but we proved ourselves. Then they trusted us. We made no errors and the Japs never broke our code."

"You were a very good soldier, then," Mackenzie said. "What is your name?"

"I am Bisahalani. I come from Alamogordo to die here."

"Whoa, whoa, what's this now?" Gravel asked.

Bisahalani gazed up at Gravel as if just noticing him for the first time. "I come to die here where my father's father's father died."

"Bullshit. You ain't gonna die, old man," Gravel said. "Mac'll take damn good care of ya, don't you worry."

"I will die. Where is my box?" the old man said, struggling to get up from the couch. "My box is out there...on the porch...please get it."

Gravel stepped outside and brought in a rectangular object, approximately a foot high and two feet wide, and weighing twenty pounds. It had mirrored panels lined with silver, turquoise and other precious stones.

"What is this?" Gravel asked.

"Infinity Box," Bisahalani said. "I made these and sold them in my shop. But no more. I am tired."

Mackenzie carefully took the Infinity Box from Gravel. "It's very heavy," she said. "Did you carry it all the way?"

"I carry it," Bisahalani said. "It is my dying gift to you, to both of you."

Mackenzie peered inside and gasped, "Oh, my, it is incredible! It goes on and on forever. Henry, you must look inside." The old man's creation was a sort of artwork, a series of cascading mirrors within a decorative box that allowed those who looked inside to see their image reflected an infinite number of times.

"Your image into infinity," Bisahalani said. "We are all into infinity, into the Great Mystery." Bisahalani gazed sadly and lovingly into the fire.

"My birth was in *Ni"Alnii'gi*, meaning Earth's Center," he continued. "My youth was in *Tsetacheechih*, the Wind Going Through the Rocks. The people there are rich mystery hanging on in towns of truth - Tewa, Sichomovi, Walpi, Polacca, the Mesas, Old Oraib," he trailed off.

Gravel and Mackenzie waited for a completion of thought and sentence but none came. The old Indian continued to stare into the fire.

"Let us help you," Mackenzie said. "We will give you food or anything you need."

"What I need is to die in peace." He closed his eyes, sucked in a raspy breath, and spread his trembling arms wide as if to sweep the world into his bosom.

Then he spoke again, "We still battle for the Earth. The mines and factories revel in their greed, seeking to steal and destroy all that remains. There is little water in my old home land, this has always been true. Hundreds of years ago, the Hopi dry farmed with windbreakers to grow food with very little water. They raised beans, corn, melons, and squash for their families and communities. But now, the miners steal away even what little water remains. The land grows more barren, the farms and villages cannot survive, and our way of life continues to crumble and disappear from the Earth. All of this so that corrupt politicians and industries can fill their pockets with more dollars."

Mackenzie placed her hand tenderly on the old man's chest and said something Gravel could not decipher.

"Soon, all will understand technology," Bisahalani continued. "But no one will know how to farm or weave. Science alters the food and soon we will have no *real* corn or beans. We will have the super Wal-Mart, but no

Hogan, no Sundance. Yes, we will have the mighty dollar, but no myth, no history, no faith, and no hope. Look in the box and you will see the answer."

"For the love of the dollar men destroy their world and themselves," Mackenzie whispered.

Dumbfounded and entranced, Gravel studied the surprising woman who shared his hideaway.

Staring up at the ceiling and beyond with glassy eyes, Bisahalani continued, "Beneath the concrete cities and asphalt highways, the forgotten forests and the lonely prairies wait silently. Too many people see only surface and not substance. They see sparkle but not depth. They do not recognize the richness of the ordinary world around them and beneath their feet. My tongue is slipping and my words hard to form. I am tired. I have said my last. Thank you for bringing me in to die by the fire."

The Indian's head seemed to quiver rapidly and his breathing grew labored. He looked up at Gravel once more and said, "You are *jeshoo*...tribulation is the only wind upon which your wings will soar."

Then he gripped Mackenzie's hand tightly, and to her he said, "Please bury me beneath the tree by the big rocks."

Mackenzie nodded as he closed his eyes and breathed no more.

"Damn," Gravel said.

■ ■ ■ ■ ■

In the morning the sky was clear and the storm was gone. The sun hung like an ostentatious orb, casting down shimmering rays of warmth upon the Texas dirt, mesquite and cactus flowers. Ants, beetles and lizards scurried out to see the sight of a Cajun burying an Indian beneath a Live Oak near the big rocks.

26

If I'd only had an extra hundred million dollars lying around, I could have bid on Gravel's mansion. But as it was, Addie and I were forced to move out of the luxurious home where we'd lived for the past year. And she was none too happy about it.

"This really sucks," Addie said, as we checked into our room at the Marriott Hotel in Brentwood, Tennessee, just a few miles south of downtown Nashville.

"Yeah, going from 40,000 square feet down to 200 will take a little getting used to," I said with a chuckle.

"I don't see how you can find any of this funny," Addie grumbled.

"Oh, come on, Addie, it's just for a little while," I said. "Look at it as an adventure."

"How are we going to party?" she asked indignantly. "We can't party in a hotel; they'll throw us out. And what are we going to do for weed and alcohol? Gravel always had plenty stocked up for emergencies."

"Calm your jets," I said. "First of all, we'll find a house or apartment to rent soon enough. I've been looking at a couple of places. Secondly, I have a little money put aside, so we're not going to starve. And, thirdly, this may come as a shock to you, but life isn't all about partying. Maybe you should think about getting a job."

Addie gave me an icy glare.

"What?" I said. "You're too good to work?"

"You are such a smartass," Addie said hatefully, before changing the subject. "You know, if we could find Gravel, neither one of us would ever have to work again."

"What do you mean?"

"I just saw on Twitter that there's a million dollar reward for anyone who finds him."

"Seriously?" I said. "A million dollars?"

"That's what it says." Addie put her pinkie finger up to her cheek, and did her best Austin Powers impression, "One *million* dollars!"

"Who's offering the reward?"

"Looks like some different people went together on it," Addie said, as she worked her phone for more information. "I think that Trump guy with the weird hair put up a bunch of money. And some lady named Roseanne and some women's rights groups or something. I don't know who else for sure."

I plopped down on the bed. "Wow, that is so crazy. Does it say why they're doing it?"

"They say he's a criminal and shouldn't be able to get away with abusing women."

I laid back and rubbed my head. "That blows my mind. It never occurred to me that someone might put up a reward for him."

Addie hopped on the bed and straddled me playfully. "If we do some more digging and calling around, maybe we could find him ourselves and get the million dollars. He must have told someone where he was going. Can't you think of anyone else to call or anywhere else to check?"

"I just don't know," I muttered. "Gravel never really gave much information about his family, other than to say how much he hated them. I think his parents and grandparents are dead, and as far as I know, he didn't have any brothers or sisters."

127

"What about cousins, aunts or uncles?" Addie asked as she nuzzled my ear and giggled. "Hey, maybe I can inspire you to think harder."

"Yeah, or maybe you'll make me forget all about Gravel Gold," I laughed. "At least for a little while."

Her long strands of dark hair danced on my face as she kissed me long and deep. Passion took control, we pulled off our clothes, and our bodies became like one.

Suddenly, right in the middle of things, it hit me.

"His aunt," I said.

Addie stopped and gave me a weird look. "What did you say?"

"I just thought of something. Remember when we were driving through Pennsylvania after the concert in Central Park? Gravel mentioned he had an aunt – or maybe it was a great-aunt – who took care of him when he was a little kid."

"Hmm, that does sound familiar," Addie said, scrunching up her face and thinking hard. "Oh, yeah, I think I remember him saying something about that, but I was really wasted at the time. Bummer."

I sat up abruptly and concentrated. "You know, I think I met her once about ten years ago, back in the early days. It seems like we were on a tour bus, going through little backwoods towns somewhere in the middle of the night."

"Well, where was it?" Addie asked impatiently.

Naked, I jumped up and paced back and forth in the small hotel room, sorting through distant, foggy memories. "I'm just not sure. But since Gravel and his family are from Louisiana, maybe that's where she lived too."

"That would make sense," Addie said. "Gravel told a lot of stories about life down there in the swamp."

"I just wish I could remember her name or something else about that night, but it's all so fuzzy. Of course, what are the odds she's even still alive? She looked really old back then, probably at least eighty or ninety."

Addie laughed.

"What's so funny?" I asked.

She pointed at my groin area and said, "Be careful, you might hurt someone with that thing."

I gave her a droll look and a deadpan laugh. "Ha, ha."

She crawled toward me on the bed like a cat, and said, "Why don't you let me take care of that and then maybe you'll be able to think clearer."

"It's worth a try," I said, and tumbled back into the bed with her.

27

She could hear the song start and stop over and over again in Gravel's room, and each stoppage was accompanied by an ever-louder burst of enraged vulgarity. Mackenzie went to the door, hesitated, then knocked. This drew an expletive-lathered response from Gravel Gold.

"Henry, please open the door," Mackenzie said.

The door opened and Gravel stood there with an electric guitar hanging at his waist. He was disheveled, unshaven, shirtless and angry. "What is it?" he said.

"I am concerned about you," Mackenzie said. "You have been closed up in here for twenty straight hours. You must take a break."

"I'll tell ya what I *must* do - I *must* get this goddamn part right," Gravel snapped.

"Perhaps you could be more like the mountain lion," Mackenzie suggested.

Gravel snapped at her remark. "Don't ever talk to me about no damn lion! I don't wanna hear nothin' about lions ever again."

Mackenzie took Gravel's hand gently in hers, and spoke calmly and soothingly, "You are tired and frustrated, yet you stubbornly continue to thrash away at your objective. The mountain lion is a clever ambush predator. It does not rush its prey head on, but rather, uses stealth."

"What the hell are ya talkin'about?"

"I'm suggesting you step away from your prey for a bit. Observe it from a distance and watch it through the brush and trees. Then when the time is right, strike with wisdom and power."

Gravel put his head in his hands with a sigh, and ran his fingers wearily through his thick, black hair.

"You have had nothing to eat or dr--" Mackenzie said, catching herself as she noted scores of empty beer and whiskey bottles scattered about the room. "Well, you have had nothing to eat for a very long time. Come to the kitchen and I will prepare some food. Please come."

As if in a trance, Gravel followed her into the kitchen, and sat down at the table now graced by a vase of wildflowers. Mackenzie gave him a mug of coffee and he sipped at it, as he watched her glide quietly around the room like a spirit, back and forth from cabinet to counter to stove, pulling dishes and utensils from drawers and doors. Gravel was transfixed by her soothing voice and calming presence as she sifted flour, cracked eggs, sliced potatoes, shredded cheese, and whisked batter.

"The coffee is good?" Mackenzie asked, breaking the silence.

"Mmm, real good," Gravel nodded. "So I guess Benji boy brought everythin' ya needed?"

"He did. Thank you very much for seeing to it."

"Ya sure got the kitchen organized. Hell, the whole damn house, for that matter."

"A place for everything, and everything in its place," Mackenzie said.

"My great-aunt Anna Marie used to say that all the time when I was a boy."

"You were close to her?"

"Yeah, I guess so. Never had no kids of her own. I was her only nephew and she sorta' kept her eye on me as best she could."

"What of your mother and father?"

"Dead," Gravel murmured.

"I'm sorry," Mackenzie said. "When did you lose them?"

"Not soon enough."

Mackenzie gently placed a plate of food before him and said, "Here, eat. It will do you good."

"Damn, looks and smells delicious," Gravel said. "What is it?"

"I have prepared mild Chile Rellenos stuffed with basted pork, raisins, and finely diced potatoes among many other things. It has some spice to it, but not too much for your empty stomach. It will invigorate you and spark your creativity."

Gravel bit into it and savored the exotic and startling blend of flavors. "My god," he said. "Ain't never tasted nothin' like this."

"You like it?"

"It's fu – I mean freakin' incredible. Sorry, almost used a little Portuguese there."

"Portuguese?"

Gravel merely shook his head at Mackenzie as if to say *Never mind*. He was smiling, relishing the exquisite taste, making the sounds of pleasure with his mouth stuffed full of food.

Later, after they'd eaten, Mackenzie asked, can you teach me to play something on the guitar?"

"I ain't much of a teacher, Mac," Gravel said.

"You have been playing guitar for many years, have you not?" Mackenzie asked.

"Sure, since I was a kid."

"And you are a very accomplished musician?"

"One of the best."

"Then simply share with me the basics of what you know. Surely you can do that," Mackenzie reasoned.

"I don't think I got the patience for teachin' somebody. In case ya ain't noticed, patience ain't one of my specialities."

Mackenzie picked up one of Gravel's acoustic guitars and put her fingers on the neck, attempting to hold down the strings. "How does one learn which strings to hold down and in which positions?"

"Mac, you are one helluva pushy woman."

Mackenzie pressed the fingers of her left hand against the strings in random positions, and strummed the guitar forcefully with her right. The result was an annoying mixture of clunks, buzzes and notes that did not belong together. She tried again and again. "How am I doing?" she asked.

"Sounds like two cats screwin'," Gravel said.

Mackenzie moved her left hand to a new position and tried again.

Gravel laughed, put his hands over his ears and said, "Now it sounds like a third cat joined in, and they're doin' it ménage a feline trios."

Mackenzie laughed with him because it sounded funny, though she wasn't quite sure what he meant.

"Look, Mac, ya got to put your fingers in the right place." Gravel picked up another guitar and demonstrated a basic D major chord. "Now, t' start with, see how I got my third finger on the high E string? Well, 'course you don't know which strings are which, do ya?"

Mackenzie made a confused face and shook her head no.

"Watch me," Gravel said. "I put my third finger on the bottom string where the second fret is."

"What is a fret?"

"Tell ya what," Gravel said, moving over and kneeling beside her. "Let me just help ya. Loosen your fingers, let 'em be limber and I'll put 'em where they go."

133

He carefully positioned each of her fingers on the neck of the guitar. "Push down hard as ya can so the strings don't buzz when you play. Now, strum the strings with the pick."

A fairly clear D chord resonated through the small room. Mackenzie's face lit up. "I did it! It sounded beautiful, didn't it?"

"Yes," Gravel said. "Absolutely beautiful."

"Teach me another."

"I had a feelin' you was gonna say that."

28

"Are we in some sort of trouble?" I asked.

"I don't know, Mr. Trotter," the police officer said, standing at the door of our hotel room. "Have you done anything wrong?"

"Well, no, of course not," I answered.

"Then you have nothing to be worried about."

"Do I have to go too?" Addie asked.

"Yes, the Special Investigator wants to talk to both of you. If all goes well, we'll have you back to your room in a few hours."

"If all goes well?" Addie said nervously. "What does that mean?"

"Yeah, what *does* that mean?" I asked.

"Just come with us," the officer said politely.

"Where are we going?" I asked.

"The Metro Government Office Building downtown. They just want to ask you a few questions."

"Who does?"

The officer gave me an irritated look, but decided to show a little more patience with us. "There are specially-appointed investigators waiting there to question you."

"I guess they want to talk about Gravel," Addie said.

The officer nodded and smiled with a touch of condescension. "In all probability, yes, ma'am."

Addie and I rode in the back seat of an unmarked police car with the officer and his partner in the front.

"Are you scared?" Addie whispered.

"No, of course not," I answered. "A little nervous, maybe, but not scared. We haven't done anything, and we don't know anything."

"Yeah, but what if they think we do? Can they put us in jail if they suspect of us something?"

I shook my head. "No, they can't do that."

"Well, this really sucks," Addie complained. "I don't think they should be allowed to do this."

"Just relax," I said. "I'm actually surprised it took this long for them to bring us in for official questioning. I mean, a detective talked to everyone in the mansion right after Gravel disappeared, but I expected them to push a little harder than they did."

■ ■ ■ ■ ■

Inside the Metro Building, we were greeted by two, friendly investigators, a man and a woman, who reminded me of detectives straight off of some television cop show. In an obvious attempt to gain our favor, they offered us a Coke and some chips. I politely declined, but Addie, of course, was more than happy to receive.

"I thought you were nervous," I whispered.

"Yeah, being nervous makes me thirsty."

"And hungry too?" I said sarcastically.

"A girl's got to eat."

After a few minutes, they split us up. The female investigator, Ms. Simpson, guided Addie into one office, and the man, Mr. Buckner, took me into another.

"Please, have a seat," Mr. Buckner said. "Are you comfortable? Can I get you anything else?"

"I'm fine, thank you," I said.

"Now, as I understand it, and please correct me if I'm wrong," Mr. Buckner began. "You are not only the guitarist in Gravel Gold's band, but also his best friend."

"Yes, that's right. I mean, I am his guitarist and bandleader; but as for being his best friend, well, I don't know about that. It's not like that's something we ever talk about or say out loud, you know."

"But it's safe to say you're very close to him."

I sort of shrugged a bit and said, "Ah, well, I suppose you could say that. I mean, I don't think anyone ever really gets too close to Gravel."

"He trusts you, though, doesn't he?"

"Well, obviously not as much as I thought he did," I chuckled. "Because he didn't say where he was going, or even tell me that he was leaving."

Buckner studied me and said, "Mm huh....okay...so then, you believe he just took off on his own?"

"Well, yeah, that's kinda what I figured."

"Did Mr. Gold have any enemies?"

"Of course," I laughed. "Gravel was famous for rubbing people the wrong way, and there was always somebody pissed at him."

"Anyone that you think might have wanted to harm him?"

I straightened up in my seat and said, "You mean, like, seriously hurt him, like, kill him?"

The investigator nodded.

"Well, there were plenty of times that we were in some tight scrapes over the years – Gravel has a knack for getting into those – you know, like bar fights or dangerous crowd scenes, stuff like that. And of course, we saw a few wacky fans that made us nervous; especially that woman in Pennsylvania who threatened us with a gun...you know, the Buffay woman."

Buckner switched topics. "Tell me about what happened the night before Gravel Gold disappeared."

"Nothing to tell, really," I said. "We were sitting up late, talking and drinking. He was drinking a lot of Jim Beam like he always does."

137

"He didn't act any different than normal? Nothing strange about his behavior?"

I gave a little laugh. "Everything about Gravel Gold is strange."

"Did he seem worried about anything?"

I thought about it. "Truth is, he was really down that night. He kept musing about how things used to be. I tried to encourage him, you know, just be there as his friend and give a listening ear. But he was pretty bummed out."

"He didn't mention any plans or trips he might be taking soon? Nothing at all?"

I shook my head. "No, nothing. He was just really, *really* down. Of course, you couldn't blame him; his whole world was falling apart, you know? The whole thing with Jazz and Gigi...and the dead lion...and the lawsuits and all those people camped out around the mansion. That's an awful lot of stress for one man to bear. Jeez, it's a wonder he was holding up at all."

"Mm huh, mm huh..." Buckner nodded. "Do you remember the last thing he said to you that night?"

I thought hard about that for a long minute. "Oh, yeah, I remember he said something about Lake Pontchartrain..."

"What does that mean?" Buckner asked.

"Let me think for a minute," I said, rubbing my temples.

"Yeah, he said he hadn't figured out what he was going to do yet, but when he did, it would be something big, like a meteor hitting Lake Pontchartrain. Yeah, that was it; I remember now."

"Alright, Mr. Trotter," Buckner said. "We appreciate your help with this. We'll be in touch. In the meantime, here's my card...you call me immediately if you hear from Mr. Gold, or if you remember any other pertinent information."

In the lobby, I met back up with Addie who seemed to be in fine spirits. "So, how did your 'interview' go?" I asked.

"Oh, it was cool," she said. "Ms. Simpson was chill, and she brought me some pizza."

"I assume she asked you about Gravel, right?"

"Yeah, yeah, she did ask me some questions. I just told her that all I really knew about him was that he drank a lot, loved to party, and could be totally off the hook sometimes."

I shook my head at my cute but silly girlfriend.

"Oh, and I told her that I wished I could find Gravel myself so I could get that one million dollars."

At the front desk, an officer informed us that he would transport us back to our hotel. As we exited the building, I caught a glimpse of a bespectacled, thin man wearing a pinkish sweater vest. He was being hurried inside by two officers, followed by several reporters, and he looked white as a ghost. It was Benjamin Wallows.

29

"Ya know, Mackenzie, I ain't laid one finger on ya the whole time ya been here," Gravel said.

Mackenzie was sitting in the straight back chair at the kitchen table. She looked up at Gravel and smiled. "You have been a perfect gentleman."

"Ain't nobody ever called me that before. And it sure ain't been easy. You're a damn pretty woman."

Gravel touched her silky, black hair, leaned over and kissed her softly on the lips.

Mackenzie did not kiss him back, yet she did not pull away. She sat perfectly still and straight, her dark eyes wide, studying his, peering into his soul.

"Ya ought to come with me," Gravel whispered.

"Where are you going?" Mackenzie said.

"Back to civilization. It won't be much longer, maybe a week. The record's almost done. Just workin' on the final mixes."

"What will you do then?" Mackenzie asked.

"Then? Then, I'm gonna take this frickin' world by its throat. I'll be back on top, bigger than ever, bigger than anybody ever dreamed of."

"That is important to you?" Mackenzie said it more as a statement than a question.

"There ain't nothin' more important than that," Gravel said. "Nothin'."

140

"So you truly were a famous singer before you came here?"

"Hell, yeah. Sold more records than anybody. Put on the biggest concert in the world. I had it all, Mac."

"You must have been very happy," Mackenzie said.

Her statement took Gravel by surprise and he looked sideways at her. "Of course I was. Why wouldn't I a' been? I had everything, every damn thing a man could want."

Gravel paused for a long moment before adding, "*Almost* everything."

Mackenzie nodded dubiously, sipped her tea, and thought for a while. "No, I will not go with you," she said finally.

"Ya can't just stay out here by yourself," Gravel said.

"Play me your newest song," Mackenzie said, changing the subject. "The one you were working on last night, the one about God."

"You're the damn stubbornest woman I ever met, and the most complicated."

"Thank you," Mackenzie said with a big smile. "Please play me your song."

"Alright, woman," Gravel said. He started toward the recording room, to play the mix for her that he'd completed on a song titled 'Sometimes All.'

"No, not that way," Mackenzie said. "I want to hear it on your guitar, just you and the guitar, natural and real, the way music should be."

"Alright, alright," Gravel said, disappointed. He'd wanted her to hear the masterpiece in all its glory, with its layers of guitar, drum, bass, keyboard and vocal tracks. But he strapped on his guitar and sang:

> *Sometimes all you got,*
> *Don't turn out like ya thought,*
> *It ain't the way ya dreamed it as a kid,*

141

Sometimes all ya need
Is a little shelter from all the greed,
And a chance to undo the wrongs ya did.

Sometimes friends forsake you,
And the world tries to break you,
To make you question
The path you choose to trod,
Sometimes all you got left is God.

Sometimes ya get confused
Twisted, torn and bruised,
And all ya really need is time to grieve,
Sometimes all it really takes,
Is a steady hand on the brakes,
To slow this freight train down,
Stop and breathe.

Sometimes it all comes down,
To one tiny sound,
The voice of God whispers in the dark.
Hallelujah, hallelujah, hallelujah,
Sometimes all you got left is God,
Hallelujah, hallelujah, hallelujah,
Sometimes all you got left is God.

"Do you truly realize what a gift you have, Henry?" Mackenzie said.

"I ain't got no damn gift," Gravel said as he tore the neck wrapper off a fresh fifth of bourbon. "'Unless ya call sadness a gift."

"But you said you were happy."

"Yeah, well, what the hell is happy? I ain't never known happy or anybody that really was."

142

"Do you even listen to your own songs, to their messages?" Mackenzie pleaded.

"I don't know," Gravel said. "I just write 'em and sing 'em, I guess. I'm not much on talkin' or thinkin' about this kind of stuff."

The moon was full and the future was empty like a bucket begging for water, like a blank sheet of paper waiting for someone to write something, anything at all.

Ghostlike and ethereal, a voice outside drifted in on the moonbeams, "Mackenzie...Mackenzie."

There is nothing worse than the sadness a man feels when he loses something he thought he'd never find, something inside himself he didn't even know was there. That very sadness seeped into the house, carried in by the stranger's voice from outside.

And just like that, Gravel somehow knew who it was. That part of him attuned to the Cajun swamp and cosmic voodoo awareness knew as surely as the sun sets in the west. "That must be your husband," he said quietly and matter-of-factly.

"Yes," Mackenzie said.

Gravel stood up and moved slowly out onto the porch. "She's in here," he called into the darkness.

The man walked slowly up the steps. He was haggard after many days in the Texas wasteland searching for his runaway wife. "I must see her," he said.

Gravel studied the man for a very long moment, peering deeply into his eyes and wondering why life had to be so cruel. The weight of ten thousand sleepless nights and the immeasurable sorrow of a broken heart welled up in Gravel Gold. In an instant, he slugged the man in the mouth with all his might, and sent him spiraling off the top step and backward into the darkness. The earth was spinning at twenty-four thousand miles per hour and it reached up to catch the young Indian.

The moon almost seemed to smile as Mackenzie cried out, "Lucas."

She ran past Gravel – who reached for her in vain – and knelt beside the man in the Texas dirt, just as a thousand other women over the centuries have knelt beside wounded men they loved.

Lucas whispered, "Mackenzie, I was a fool and I'm so very sorry. Please forgive me."

She cradled his head against her bosom, dabbed the blood from his face with a tissue, and said, "Of course."

Behind them, Gravel slammed the door closed.

In the end, it's not who you are that matters…it's who loves you.

Part Three

30

As soon as the police officer dropped us off at our hotel, Addie and I packed a few things and jumped on I-40 West, destination Shreveport, Louisiana. I was determined to make the nine hour trip in seven.

"So what's the plan once we get there?" Addie asked.

"I'm hoping we'll find some Lamartinieres down there who are related to Gravel, or somebody who has an idea on where he might be."

"How are we going to do that?"

"We'll ask around, look in the local phone book, or even check courthouse records if we have to."

"You think it'll work?"

"It's worth a shot," I said. "All the reporters and tabloids have probably already tried this, but maybe we'll get lucky and find Gravel's great-aunt...that is, if she's even still alive. Like I said before, she was really old when I met her."

The next day in Shreveport we mingled and chatted up folks in cafes, coffeehouses, markets, and other gathering places in various parts of the small city. The main thing we learned was that many reporters had indeed come calling long before we did, and they had apparently dug up nothing of value. Everybody seemed to agree that Gravel was raised in the swamps on the outskirts of the city, and that Gravel and his daddy wrestled gators, but we were given conflicting answers regarding exactly where this all happened. But they were proud of their home town hero, in spite of his legal troubles and the accusations being made against him.

"Maybe his family moved around a lot when he was a kid, like from swamp to swamp, you know," Addie suggested.

"Yeah, that could be," I said.

"So where are we going now?" Addie asked.

"The Post Office," I answered as I pulled the car into the parking lot. "Might be a good place to borrow a phone book and ask some questions. Who would know more about the names and addresses of people in Shreveport than the local postal workers?"

We caught it at a good time; the place was nearly empty. The lady at the counter let us borrow a phone book, and we opened it up and turned to the "L" section.

An old man wearing a postal uniform wandered over to us and asked, "Who are ya lookin' for? I been here all my life, so I pretty much know anybody they is to know."

"We're looking for anyone named Lamartiniere," I said.

The man looked us over and leaned on the counter. "You ain't one of them reporters, are you? I can always spot 'em, and I can tell you ain't got that newspaper look about you."

"No, we're not reporters."

"But you're looking for Gravel Gold, ain't you?"

I nodded. "Yes, that's right."

"You look familiar to me. You a musician?"

"I play guitar for Gravel, and I guess you might say I'm one of his best friends."

"Me, too," Addie chimed in.

The man smiled. "Best friends, but you don't know where he is. Life sure is a funny road, ain't it?"

"I'm worried about him," I said. "I don't know why he took off without telling anyone, and I decided I'd sat

148

around on my rear end long enough. I had to get out and start looking for him."

"So here we are," Addie said.

The old man nodded. "And here you are."

There was a long awkward silence, and I looked back down at the phone book.

The man said, "Gravel's family was dirt poor, but I always knew that boy was going to make it big. I could just tell. He had this way about him, this…"

"Swagger," I said.

"Yeah, that's it," the man said. "You just never knew what he might do next. To be honest, he was a little bit scary, him and his daddy, both."

"Then he hasn't changed at all since he was a kid," Addie said.

The man smiled big and wide. "You hit that nail dead on, young lady."

"About ten years ago," I said. "We came through here on a tour bus, and Gravel stopped in to see his great aunt. I'm just wondering if she's still…you know, still alive."

The man nodded slowly and spoke softly, "Anna Marie Lamartiniere."

"Yes, that sounds right," I said. "I'm pretty sure that was her name."

"Well, this is your lucky day," the man said with a very serious look. "I can give you some inside information that hardly anybody knows about. This is just between us; can I trust you?"

"Yes, we won't tell a soul," I said, and leaned in close to the old man.

"My youngest daughter is a nurse, and a real good one," he whispered. Then he raised his eyebrows high and said, "And just who do you think she takes care of every day?"

Addie said, "Gravel's aunt?"

"Bingo," the man said.

149

31

Gravel Gold was alone in the old farmhouse, and the ghost of his great-great uncle whispered through the smoky Marlboro haze as though it was taunting him in his alcoholic rage.

Gravel pressed 'Play' on the console and stood in the center of the room with his arms spread wide. The tracks rolled over him at full volume, the power and glory lifting him as nothing else ever had or ever would lift him again.

Look out for the rocks,
They're way too close for comfort,
The wind has blown me far off course,
I beat my head against unmovable objects,
Man, I'm a victim of my own stubborn force.

I've been lost in the eye of the hurricane,
That some people like to call love,
The sea was raging and I had no choice,
But to trust the stars above.

This battered old ship's been lost at sea,
Wind and waves crashing over me,
But I'll throw my anchor down
On this long, lonely trip,
If you'll come aboard this battered old ship.

The further I go, the closer I get,
To being further away from my home,
I may rule in the kingdom of my heart,
But I'm tired, tired of living here all alone.

Yes, this battered old ship
Needs a port for the night,
Someone to say, "It's alright,"
And I'll throw my anchor down
On this long, lonely trip,
If you'll come aboard this battered old ship,
Please come aboard this battered old ship.

The song ended and faded into the massive silence of the tumbleweed prairie. Gravel wiped tears from his eyes and smiled a smile as big as a politician's lie. He stood there entranced in the stillness until one of his burner phones broke the spell.

Gravel answered it with a whispered, "Yeah."

"Mr. Gold, it's me, Benjamin."

"You okay, Benji?"

"No, not really. I'm so sorry but I can't be there tomorrow as planned."

"Why not?"

"They're watching me, following me--"

"Who's following you?" Gravel asked. "Who and what are ya talkin' about?"

"The police, reporters, crazy fans, everybody thinks I know where you are."

Gravel laughed. "Well, ya do, don't ya?"

"Well, yes, but..." Benjamin's voice trailed off for a moment. "They took me in and questioned me for hours, and treated me like some sort of criminal. And they're doing the same thing to everyone in your circle and mine. I'm afraid your location will soon be compromised, if it hasn't been already. They could be on their way out there right now, for all we know."

"Benji, my boy, you've got calm down and relax," Gravel said softly, "It doesn't matter now. The end is near."

"What do you mean?"

"The new record's done. I have all the tracks ready to give to the world. In just a few days, I'm goin' home."

"Is Miss Mackenzie coming with you?"

There was silence for a while and just when Benjamin thought he'd lost the connection, Gravel said, "I don't know anybody by that name."

32

We were greeted at the door by Nurse Dottie, the primary care-giver for Anna Marie Lamartiniere. "Hello, you must be Trotter and Addie. My brother called and told me about you. Please come inside."

"Thank you, Dottie," I said. "We really appreciate you letting us visit. We won't take but just a moment of your time."

"Happy to have you; we don't get many friendly visitors. Most of them are reporters or gold diggers or scavengers just trying to get a story or some memorabilia so they can sell it on eBay or something such as that."

"I'm sorry to hear that," I said. "I'm sure it's hard being related to a superstar."

"And especially now that he's missing and so many people are trying to find him," Addie added.

"So true, young lady," Dottie said. "Now let me tell you about Miss Lamartiniere. I told her she was getting visitors, and that you're in Henry's band. That's his real name, you know."

"Yes, ma'am," I said.

"Now she's in the back room prettying herself up for company – she does love to get friendly visitors! But please understand that she's 95 years old now, and she gets real forgetful. And sometimes she tends to get a little mixed up and repeats herself. So, try not to let it bother you; just smile and nod."

The back room was extremely large, and had dozens of shelves lined with hundreds of picture frames and photo albums documenting the Lamartiniere family history. Henry Lamartiniere, also known as Gravel Gold, was, of course, featured prominently in many of these. There were also country quilts draped over the furniture, and glass figurines and knick-knacks on tables and bookcases. A family Bible the size of Rhode Island sat prominently on the coffee table, and on the walls were pictures of The Lord's Supper, Jesus on the cross, the Rapture, and the stoning of Stephen.

Miss Lamartiniere was a tiny, white-haired woman with a never-ending smile. She wore a pretty print dress and a white sweater, with grey-blue eyes that were crisp and cheerful behind silver frames. She greeted us warmly, "Hello, hello, please sit down and visit. Dottie will you get us some sweet tea and some sandwiches?"

"Oh, that's okay," I said. "You don't need to bother with anything like that."

"Oh, pish posh. You have to eat," Miss Lamartiniere said. She pointed at Addie. "I bet you're hungry."

"Sure, yeah," Addie said. "Thanks."

I laughed. "She's always hungry."

"Well, look at her; she's skinny as a rail," Miss Lamartiniere said. "You have to eat more, sweetie, or you'll wither away to nothing." Then she turned her attention toward me and said," Oh, lordy, I think I remember you. Didn't you stop to visit me one night with Henry years ago? Weren't you in his band?"

"Yes, ma'am, I play guitar in Gra—in Henry's band."

Miss Lamartiniere continued, "We don't get many friendly visitors around here. Did you meet Dottie? She's my angel, she surely is. She's real good people...always taking care of me, making sure I take my

154

medicines and such as that. She's like my own daughter, of course, I never had children of my own, 'cept I do count Henry as my own, you know."

She paused for a moment to catch her breath before pressing on, "Now where are you folks from? Are you just passing through here or are you planning to be in Shreveport for a spell? It's a fine town, but it's a lot bigger than it was when I was a girl. Lord, I remember when Henry was a young'un. Sometimes that boy could be mean as a snake, but he had a good heart, I always knew he did. Deep down inside, he was as fine a boy as you could ever want."

"Miss Lamartiniere," I began tentatively. "Have you seen or heard from Henry recently?"

"No, no, I can't say that I have. What's it been, Dottie, a year or so since we heard from Henry?"

"Yes, Miss Lamartiniere, it was about a year ago," Dottie said.

"Oh, but Henry don't have much time for talking or visiting nowadays. He's done real well for himself; he's a big country music star, probably the most famous one in the whole world. I'm so proud of him I could just bust. I always knew he was goin' to be something special. Now everybody in the world knows about Gravel Gold, but of course, he'll always be just Henry to me. I was the closest thing to a momma that boy ever had, and he's just like my own son."

"Well, ma'am, we're just trying to catch up with Henry," I said. "He took off for a little vacation, and we don't know where he is at the moment. We were hoping maybe you--"

"Oh, my, that boy used to run off and couldn't find him for days at a time," Miss Lamartiniere said, rambling on. "I used to set that sweet boy right there on my knee and bounce him up and down when he wasn't no bigger than a tadpole." She tapped her knee to mark the very

155

spot where the bouncing had occurred.

"But that poor child was stuck with a runaway momma and a no-account daddy," Miss Lamartiniere continued. "It broke my heart, I swear it did. The Lord knows how many times I prayed for that family, but the Devil tore them apart. Henry's daddy drank all the time, and before you knew it, Henry was drinking too. He wasn't no more than ten years old, and he was already getting drunk. I'll tell you right now, I don't approve of alcohol. It's a sin is what it is, plain and simple, and it ruins a person's life. I'm ninety-five years old, and in all them years I ain't never seen one person that was made better by drinking. I guarantee you that. Alcohol is a tool of the Devil."

Dottie came back in with iced tea, brownies, and servings of green salad. "Miss Lamartiniere, would you like to say grace?"

Anna Marie bowed her head and prayed, "Heavenly Father, we thank Thee for this beautiful day that Thou hast given to us, and for this food of which we can partake. Please bless it to the nourishment of our bodies. We pray for them that's in need in these troublesome times in our country. And we pray for our President, that you will give him wisdom to solve our problems. Thank you, Lord, for these fine young people that have come to visit. Please bless them and watch over them. And I pray that if either of them's not been saved, that they will accept the Lord Jesus Christ into their hearts before it's everlastingly too late. We pray all this in Jesus name. Amen."

Addie and I mumbled a polite "Amen."

"I made the green salad myself," Miss Lamartiniere said proudly. "Dottie does most of my cookin', but I still make the green salad."

"I can't make it like she does," Dottie conceded.

"Been makin' it for eighty-two years," Anna Marie said. "Reckon I ought to be pretty good at it by now. Take a bite of that green salad and see if you don't like it."

I studied the serving in my plate and poked at it with my fork. It appeared to be a slurry of semi-solid lime gelatin containing clumps of cottage cheese and bits of assorted fruits and nuts. There were other indiscernible ingredients, but we smiled graciously at Ms. Lamartiniere and took a bite.

"Mmmm, it's delicious," Addie said. "It's the best green salad I've ever had." But I suspected she had never in her entire life had a green salad that even remotely resembled this one.

"Why, thank you, sweetie," Anna Marie said, affectionately squeezing Addie's arm.

"So, you say you haven't heard from Henry in a year?" I asked, trying to gently steer the conversation, hoping maybe she'd remember something.

Miss Lamartiniere paused and thought a bit. "How long's it been, Dottie, since we heard from Henry?"

"It's been about a year," Dottie answered.

"My, folks used to hound poor old Henry," Miss Lamartiniere said. "They never give him no peace. And they used to come around here all the time too. Had to get my number unpublished cause they'd call here at all hours of the day. That Enquirer magazine…and that Globe paper…oh, what was some of them other ones?"

"We called the police on them several times," Dottie offered. "They'd be knocking on our door and out in the yard taking pictures, trampling the flowers. Such a shame people don't know how to behave decently these days."

"They were always trying to dig something up about my Henry," Miss Lamartiniere said. "They even offered me money if I'd do an interview. I told 'em '*No, thank you.* I got the Lord Jesus in my heart and Henry looking

157

after me. What do I need with more money? That's exactly what I told 'em."

"Yes, those tabloids will do anything for a story," I said. "They can be very persistent."

Miss Lamartiniere continued, "You know, Henry had it rough as a cob growing up. His no-count momma run off and left him, and his daddy didn't put much effort into raising the boy."

"Yes, ma'am, he did," I said, hoping to break in and stop her from repeating the same stories once again. But it didn't work.

"Now, I know that Henry's had his troubles with the alcohol," Miss Lamartiniere said. "He's raised a ruckus sometimes, but I don't believe all them stories they tried to pin on him. No, sirree. Don't believe it for a minute. Many's the time I set him right up here on my knee and bounced him up and down, pretty as you please. Henry always was a good boy, deep down. He saw to it that I was taken care of and I never have to worry about another worldly thing. He put plenty of money aside for me, and hired Dottie and those other folks to watch over me. He's a good boy. Can't nobody tell me different."

I glanced questioningly toward Dottie. "It's true," she said. "Henry went to great lengths to take care of Ms. Lamartiniere. He hired me to stay with her, and arranged for a company to do all the upkeep on the house and lawn. Everything she needs is provided for by a very generous fund that Henry set up."

Gravel had never mentioned any of this to me.

"It sounds like he's been a wonderful nephew to you, Miss. Lamartiniere," Addie said.

"Great-nephew is what he is," the old woman said. "The only one I have. You know, my memory ain't what it used to be. It's funny how my mind works…sometimes I can't hardly remember today, but I can remember things from years ago."

"Those are the precious memories," Dottie said, gently taking Miss Lamartiniere's hand in hers.

The silence in the house was broken by the ringing of my cell phone. My phone showed 'Unknown Caller' and I decided I should take it. I excused myself, stepped a few feet away, and answered softly, "Hello."

The voice on the line shocked me; it was Gravel Gold. "Trotter?"

I was quiet for a moment before replying, "Yes."

"Where are ya?"

"Uh, well...you may not believe it..."

"Just tell me where the hell ya are."

"I'm at your aunt's place in Shreveport. I mean, your great-aunt."

Now it was his turn to be quiet.

"Addie and I were just trying to find you," I said. "We're not bothering her; we've had a real nice visit."

"Put her on the line for a minute," Gravel ordered.

I handed the phone to Miss Lamartiniere.

"Somebody wants to talk to me?" she asked, covering the phone with her hand. "Who is it? It's not one of them sales people is it? They call all the time, it seems like. They're nearly as bad as them reporters from the National Enquirer and People magazine. I swear--"

"No, no," I said quickly. "It's Henry. He wants to talk to you."

The little old lady drew in her breath sharply, "Oh, sweet Lord, my Henry's calling? Oh, my!"

"Miss Lamartiniere, please, don't keep him waiting," Dottie said, pointing at the phone.

"Henry, is that you?" Miss Lamartiniere said softly.

On the other end of the line, Gravel spoke tenderly, "Yes, Aunt Anna, it's me. How are ya feelin'? You doin' okay?"

"It's so good to hear your voice, Henry. What a blessing. I've been praying for you every day."

159

"I want ya to know I'm thinkin' about ya, and I've made sure that you'll always have everything ya need. You understand that, don't ya?"

"Oh, I know you have," Miss Lamartiniere said. "Are you coming by the house soon? We got some green salad and it's real tasty. And we can cook up some barbeque and creamed corn just the way you like it."

Gravel didn't say a word for a minute.

"You still there, Henry?"

"Yes, Aunt Anna, I'm here. Now I want ya to remember that I love ya, okay? Promise me you'll remember that."

Tears trickled down the old woman's face, and I wondered what Gravel was saying to make her cry. Addie and I exchanged troubled looks.

Finally, Miss Lamartiniere said, "I know you do, Henry. And I love you too. Just like you was my very own boy."

She handed the phone back to me and said, "He wants to talk to you again."

Nervously, I took the phone and said, "Hey, it's me."

"Be in Abilene, Texas, tomorrow afternoon at 3:00 pm," Gravel said. "I'll call ya back then. Got it?"

"Yes," I said. "We'll be there."

33

Outside San Angelo, in a dive called The Red Rooster, a jukebox muttered from the corner, spitting out bits of Patsy Cline, Willie Nelson, and Merle Haggard. The Pabst Blue Ribbon clock on the wall displayed the time to the establishment's six patrons and one bartender, none of whom was interested in the time. A shelf above the cash register sagged in the middle from years of bearing the burden of Jack, Old Granddad, Jose Cuervo, and a host of other gut-rotters from Early Times to Ancient Age.

At a quarter past half drunk, Gravel Gold sat hunched over the ratty bar staring at the names, initials, and sexual suggestions that had been carved into the wood over the years. Wearing a trench coat, sporting a well-designed, fake beard, and with his cowboy hat pulled low over his eyes, he looked more like a member of ZZ Top than he did Gravel Gold. No one in the ragged tavern had a clue who he was, and he was glad for that. The time was coming quickly when he'd be back in the front page headlines.

Thinking about Mackenzie, Gravel swirled his drink and mumbled softly to himself. A television in the corner above the bar flashed rapid-fire images and murmured endlessly with the pop music of the day. Gravel hadn't paid much attention to it, but suddenly something caught his eye, *something about Gigi.*

"Hey, bartender," Gravel said quickly, motioning toward the TV. "Would ya turn that up?"

Gravel had given very little thought to his estranged wife in the past few months, and now, here she was being interviewed on some sort of Behind-The-Music segment on the Now! Entertainment Channel. To make it worse, Shonnaveesta was on one side of her, and a caged lion was on the other. Gravel couldn't believe his eyes. He leaned toward the screen and listened closely.

The interviewer was a young, red-haired man in a bright red suit and bow tie. He reminded Gravel of a red-headed Pee-Wee Herman. The interviewer asked Gigi, "How much credit do you give to your husband, Gravel Gold, for your current success? I mean, you probably learned some things from him that helped you along the way."

"What kind of stupid question is that?" Gigi spouted. "I don't give him no damn credit at all."

Shonnaveesta piped up, though much of what she said was bleeped out, "That piece of **** didn't ever do nothin' for this girl. He ******* garbage is all he is."

"He killed my sweet Linda and he cheated on me," Gigi fumed. "Is that the kinda help you're talkin' about?"

"Gravel Gold ancient history, ginger," Shonnaveesta said. "We make the *************** music of today. 2VBW gonna ******* rock the ******** world."

"Meow, down girls, easy now…I'm on your side," the man purred, and segued into a video clip. "You certainly have had unparalleled success right out of the gate with your collaborative efforts. Let's take a quick look at a montage of your hits so far."

Gravel was mesmerized, stunned as the images raced by on the screen. Gigi and Shonnaveesta were prancing about awkwardly, attempting to dance in what appeared to be ten-inch heels. Their outrageous makeup made them look like a perverted cross between Lady Gaga, Boy

George, and Orphan Annie. And all this was interspersed with cheesy, computer-generated images of Gigi, Shonnaveesta, and a lion riding in a spaceship, playing in an NFL football game, and rowing a tiny boat across a raging sea.

After the video segment, the red-haired man asked, "Yowzee, sizzling hot stuff! So, what are your immediate plans coming off these latest successes? Back in the studio? A tour? A major vacay? Your adoring fans want to know."

"Our plan is to be, like, the biggest thing to ever hit the music scene," Gigi announced. "And I'm talkin' about, like, in forever, goin' all the way back to, like, The Spice Girls."

The red-haired man grinned into the camera, "My, that is going back a looonnnggg way!" There was a large splattering of canned studio laughter.

Gravel waved at the bartender. "Turn it off, turn the damn thing off." Then he finished off his whiskey and stared at the empty bottle, still stunned by what he'd just witnessed on the television screen.

Meanwhile, one of the cocks in the Red Rooster, a young man with a big mouth and small brain, had been seeking an opponent for a game of pool. Full of billiards bravado, he approached Gravel Gold. Gravel peered over his shoulder through bloodshot eyes, and deemed the young man not worthy of his efforts.

"No, thanks, kid," Gravel growled. "Go home to mommy."

The young man, however, wouldn't give up, wouldn't shut up. "Come on, big man. Play me. Are ya chicken shit?"

"What's your name, kid?" Gravel asked.

"Bubba."

"Bubba? Are you kiddin' me? Who the hell names their kid Bubba?"

163

"You gonna talk or play?"

Gravel said, "There ain't nothin' worse than a little man with a big mouth."

"Better'n bein' a big man with a little dick."

Gravel spun around. "All right, you asked for it, but you got about as much chance as a one-legged man in a three-legged race. Name your price, boy."

"A hundred bucks a game."

Gravel shook his head and laughed. He almost felt sorry for the punk.

Gravel Gold handled a cue stick like a toothpick when he had a sucker right where he wanted him. He beat the kid three games in a row, and was working on number four. Smooth as silk, Gravel tapped orange in the side pocket, green in the far corner, and put down the eight-ball. Game over.

"You suck," Gravel said.

"This is total bullshit!" the young man shouted, slamming his stick against the wall. His rage, which had been seething below the surface with each losing game, now found its release point. "Goddamn it to hell," he raged, pounding his fist on the table.

"Calm down, kid, and pay up," Gravel said as he turned to the bar for another drink. "And then run along home before you lose your allowance and the money from your paper route."

Bubba saw no humor in the situation. His manhood challenged and his foolish temper flaring, the kid pulled a blade from his pocket and lunged toward Gravel from behind. But this wasn't Gravel Gold's first bar fight. He dodged the slashing attack, and, in one fluid motion, grabbed the young man's arm and pushed the blade back upon his attacker. Stainless steel severed soft skin. His eyes like lunar lakes, the kid gasped and fell upon the felt of the pool table, red pouring onto green.

Gravel stood over him, smirking. All that time in seclusion, he'd really missed exhilarating escapades like this.

Sirens soon wailed as police and paramedics descended upon the dive. The young man was wounded badly, but he would live. The four witnesses in the bar gave their statements, and they all agreed that the young man had come looking for trouble. It was self-defense, plain and simple, and the official police report stated that Mr. Henry J. Lamartiniere had done what was necessary to protect himself.

There were would be no charges brought against him, but Gravel knew what would happen. Even with the fake beard, a couple of the officers had looked at him as though he seemed somehow familiar to them, but they couldn't quite put their finger on why. Gravel knew that look well. It might take only a few minutes, or it could be days, but someone would put the pieces together, or someone somewhere would spot the story, and recognize that the Henry Lamartiniere involved in this stabbing incident was indeed Gravel Gold. Then the media would descend upon San Angelo. But Gravel wasn't ready for that yet; almost, but not quite.

Gravel made a few more phone calls, then skipped town in the dark of night in a battered Chevy half-ton. With only the barest of necessities, he traveled north toward Abilene, following mostly back roads through a sinister and barren land of dirt, dust and detritus. Now that he'd set things in motion, Gravel planned to hole up in a third-rate, no-star dump of a motel – someplace where no one would find him until he wanted to be found – and wait for things to unfold. He slipped a copy of his new CD into the player and sang along with himself as he drove, wailing like the most broken-down man in the world.

With a head full 'a steam,
I'm a trackless train,
If love was a gun,
There'd be a bullet in my brain,
If I was a cloud, I think I'd rain,
Now I'm gonna rain...
Yeah, I think I'm gonna rain...
Like it ain't never rained before...

34

"This is so exciting," Addie said. "What do you think Gravel's up to?"

"I don't know," I said as we roared across the border between Louisiana and Texas, heading for Abilene at 90 mph on Interstate 20.

"I am so totally psyched right now," she said, twisting in her seat to face me. "What do you think this is about?"

"You just asked me that, babe," I said. "And I still don't know."

Addie twirled her hair and bit on her lip. "Maybe he's done a total makeover and he's going to go Metal Hip Hop or something crazy like that. What do you think?"

"Uh, still don't know," I said.

"What's wrong with you?" she asked. "Aren't you excited?"

I nodded. "Yeah, excited…and just a little nervous. The whole thing just seems so weird."

"How do you mean?"

"This whole top-secret, clandestine thing just seems so over the top to me," I said. "But whatever it is, I guess we'll find out soon enough."

Jack rabbits, oil rigs, and sagebrush watched us whiz by across flat lands of dry dirt, silt, clay, and brush. The road shot off toward the horizon straight as the arrow of God, and we chased it across the sky. A few hours later we said hello to the outskirts of Abilene.

"It's almost three o'clock," Addie observed, having been watching the clock and reminding me of the time all along. "What should we do now?"

"We wait for him to call," I said. "Just like he said."

"Think we have time to get something to eat?" Addie asked. "I'm hungry."

"We can try. Watch for a fast food place."

My phone rang.

"Oh, no," Addie said. "Now I won't get to eat."

Sure enough, it was Gravel.

"You in Abilene?" he asked.

"We're here," I answered.

"Follow the loop around to the north," he said. "Get on Highway 83 and head north. There'll be a rundown, piece-of-crap place called the Mustang Motel on your right, just a few miles up 83. I'm in Unit 107."

We were there in fifteen minutes.

The motel was worse than Gravel had described it, like a propped-up cluster of rotted boards surrounded by cigarette butts, tobacco juice spittle, and empty bottles beneath a wind-whipped maelstrom of fast-food wrappers, tattered super-market sales papers, and the stench of a thousand unjustified indignities and heart-wrenching acts of cruelty perpetrated by man upon man, and God upon man. A battered sign read: *Vaca cy*.

And there was Gravel Gold, standing in the doorway of 107, smoking a cigarette and taking in the afternoon sun with a big smile.

"Would you look at that," I said. "He looks good, surprisingly good."

"Yeah, he does," Addie said, also a bit bewildered.

"I'm not sure what I was expecting," I said. "But I guess part of me figured he'd been on a long, bad drunk spell, and he'd look like he'd been through hell."

"Me, too," Addie said. "I figured if a guy runs off like that, then he's probably really messed up, you know?"

Gravel was watching us from the doorway. "Well, let's do this before he gets pissed," I said. "He's probably wondering what we're doing just sitting here."

We got out and Gravel shouted, "Trotter, Addie, good to see ya. Come on inside and check out my fine luxury accommodations."

Addie ran over, hugged Gravel and giggled, "Sorry, but your place looks like crap."

Gravel laughed, "Yeah, but it's a pretty good deal for $39.95 a night."

"You're getting ripped off," I said. "They must have seen you coming a mile away."

Addie winked and said, "You know, those cigarettes are going to be the death of you. Maybe you should give that one to me."

"I can one hundred percent guarantee that cigarettes will not kill me," Gravel said. "But if ya want this one, girl, you're welcome to it."

"Thanks, I've been dying for one for hours," Addie said as she took a long draw. "You know Trotter doesn't like me to smoke in the car."

"It stinks up the car and it makes me nauseated," I said.

"And I'm hungry too," Addie said. "Got anything to eat?"

"Girl, you ain't changed a bit," Gravel said. "There's some hot wings and pizza left over there on the table. Better eat it before the cockroaches get to it."

Addie grabbed a box and plopped down on the unmade bed.

"Look, Gravel," I began. "It's really great to see you, but I have a thousand questions, you know? I mean, what happened to you? You just disappeared. Where were you

169

all this time? And what are you going to do now?"

"Sorry, Trots, but there's no time for question and answer," Gravel said. "Thing are happening, unfolding too fast now."

"What things?" I asked. "Can't you at least give us an idea of what's going on?"

"Let's just say I've been very, very busy...thinkin' and changin' and plannin'. I wandered in the wilderness like the children of Israel, and I was tempted and deceived like Jesus in the desert. And now, big things are about to happen."

Gravel stopped pacing and lit up another cigarette before continuing, "Benji and Charles took care of the business side of things, got all the contracts laid out proper, all of it on the down low, or course."

"So, Benji *was* in on this!" I said, not a little agitated.

"Who is Charles?" Addie interjected with her mouth full of cold pizza.

Gravel ignored us and rolled on. "But nobody else knows about any of this, so don't either of you say or email or text a single word to anyone anywhere. And none of that twittering tweet stuff either. Do you understand me? Not a single word."

Addie and I exchanged puzzled glances; neither of us had a clue what all of this meant. "Of course," I said. "Not a word."

"The Lord God works in mysterious ways, and tomorrow, my friends, all our lives are gonna be turned upside down," Gravel said, spreading his arms wide and speaking like some sort of gospel evangelist. "Twenty-four hours from now, the sun will stand still, the moon will turn to blood, and the Cajun Voodoo Man will rule the Earth."

Gravel closed his eyes and mumbled something we couldn't make out. I looked at Addie and she mouthed, "Is he praying?"

Then Gravel said, "And now I have somethin' for ya to hear, somethin' like ya ain't never heard before. Listen with your ears and your hearts. As Jesus said, *He that hath ears to hear, let him hear.*"

The hotel room where Gravel was hiding out was as old as the hills, but the sound system he'd brought with him was state-of-the-art and capable of bringing every high-hat, harmony, frequency, and nuance of a song into absolute clarity.

Gravel pushed the Play button and the first track, "Crucify You," rang out with incalculable cosmic power, like the pristine pealing of a country church bell across a field of virgin snow on a crisp Sunday morning. The song moved me as I hadn't been moved in a long time, and my eyes welled up with tears. Even Addie was stunned by the song; she held the pizza in her lap and didn't take a single bite during the entire song. The closing refrain whispered:

> *Kings and angels may fall from grace,*
> *Tears will stain your sweet face,*
> *The whole world may crumble,*
> *All your plans could fail,*
> *And they might even crucify you*
> *With a hammer and nail,*
> *They will drive it...bit by bit...*
> *They will drive it...bit by bit...*
> *Through your heart.*

Gravel opened his eyes and looked at me. I couldn't find words to adequately describe what I'd just heard, but I knew it had to be one of the greatest songs in the history of music. Gravel saw the tears in my eyes, knew exactly what I was thinking, and simply nodded his head. Then he played the second track, and the third, each one growing, building upon the previous song, creating a work of art, a masterpiece, music like it used to be, music like it was meant to be.

I never really liked to admit it, but part of me envied Gravel's incredible talent; and I was sometimes angry that he, rather than I, had been given such a gift. Everyone knew that he was a unique singer with incredible vocal range, an innovative guitarist, and a ghoulish madman on stage; and that he lived and breathed such raw intensity that he could enthrall a crowd like no one else on earth.

But now it was clear that his world-class songwriting abilities had risen to unparalleled levels of creativity. These songs were ground-breaking, new material with opposing rhythmic forces, complex syncopation, and a gritty, back-to-the-earth, organic sound. Gravel Gold had created an epic new record that would propel him back to the top of every music chart and into every front page headline in the entire world. His name would be on the tip of every person's tongue and would dominate all the artistic, music and entertainment news. Gravel Gold would be born again, and ascend from the ashes like the great Phoenix of antiquity.

35

"The life of the flesh is in the blood...
For it is the blood that maketh an atonement
for the soul."

-- Leviticus 17:11, Holy Bible, KJV

After the eighth song on the CD ended, Gravel stopped the player. "We're running out of time," he said. "We need to go to the Firehouse."

"The what?" I asked.

"Just get in my truck," Gravel said as he headed out the door.

Addie and I shrugged and followed him.

"I know the guy that owns the place," Gravel said as he started up the pickup. "His name's Bobby; I've known him for years. It's just a few miles down the road."

The Firehouse was a raucous Abilene nightspot with an unusual conglomeration of patrons: mullet-bearing rednecks, hooter-girl wannabes in short shorts, avid motorcyclists, and an edgy college crowd. With fifty-cent wings and ice-cold longnecks, it was the place to be in Abilene. No one recognized us as we waded quickly through the thick crowd in the dim bar.

We found the owner of the establishment in the back room. Gravel slapped him on the back and said, "Bobby, how the hell ya been, brother?"

Bobby's eyes went wide as the back end of a bison. "Oh, my God, Gravel Gold! Haven't seen you in years. What in the world are you doin' down here?"

"I come to see if ya need some live music to liven this joint up," Gravel said.

"Are you kidding?" Bobby said. "You wanna play some music? Here? Hell, yes. Double hell yes, my man. When you wanna do it?"

"Right now," Gravel said matter-of-factly.

"Well, rock on, my friend," Bobby said. "Want me to introduce you?"

"No, no, no," Gravel shook his head. "No introductions; this is totally on the sly. Just make sure your instruments and board are all set to go."

"We did a sound check earlier, so it's all ready," Bobby said. "You're on, brother."

"And don't worry about the damages. Ya know I'm good for every penny."

"Hell, yeah," Bobby said again, but then paused. "Wait, what?…what damages?"

"The Cajun Voodoo Man is in the zone tonight," Gravel said as he walked away. "Come on, Trotter, let's do it."

"Do what?" I asked.

"We're gonna rock this joint, Trotter. I been holdin' it in for way too long. I need one last night of the real thing, just one last night."

He'd taken me completely by surprise. "You know, you could've given me a little advance notice," I said.

Gravel laughed, "Yeah, but it's more fun this way. Besides, what's the problem? You catch stage fright while I was gone? Just follow my lead."

"Hey, what do you mean 'one last time'?"

174

Gravel ignored the question as we climbed on stage with beer bottles and dishes clanging, Texas beef sizzling on the grill, and the crowd roaring like a large, hot hive of buzzed bees.

Gravel handed me an electric guitar – a blonde 1957 Stratocaster Relic – and I gladly strapped it on. He sat at the drums and began to play, somewhat loosely and disjointedly, but I followed his meandering lead, just as I had ten thousand times before. Since we hadn't been officially introduced to the room, the crowd paid little attention to us at first – we were just background noise. But, slowly, Gravel increased the tempo and complexity of his rhythm and percussive attack, and soon we were smashing walls of sound off the walls of the room like no two-piece band ever had before.

Then Gravel began to sing and wail, tenderly yet powerfully, his voice digging at the souls of the listeners, pulling them in, winning them over. They became entranced by the mysterious drummer singing in the shadows, with his black hat pulled down low over his eyes.

Trouble ain't my middle name
It's my only name,
I don't have to cheat to win,
Cuz I don't play your game,
Don't tell me love's the answer...
It's the problem every time,
You'll get nothin' but a broken heart...
When ya lay it on the line,
You come from the Devil's seed,
My blood is what you what you need,
Cut me now, and watch me bleed.
Cut me now, and watch me bleed.

The people in the nightclub swayed as one, a swarm of spectators swept up in Gravel's sea of sorrow as he pounded the drums and repeated the mournful, mesmerizing refrain over and over again, building, rising, exploding. There was an unspeakable rage and sorrow to his performance that I'd never seen before; and the crowd, having recognized him, chanted: *Gravel Gold. Gravel Gold. Gravel Gold.*

Suddenly Gravel leaped over the drum kit to the front of the stage, and pulled the knife from his boot, just as Addie and I had seen him do that night in Pennsylvania. The crowd gasped as he raised the blade over his head, the neon lights reflecting off the cold steel.

"The Cajun Voodoo Man is here tonight!" Gravel roared. "There is power in the blood, power in the blood!" He led the entire room in several choruses of that old gospel hymn, and had everyone swaying as if fully enraptured by the Spirit of God.

Then, grinning maniacally, Gravel broke the spell by slashing the blade down his right forearm twice, making a six-inch long 'X'. He grabbed a guitar from its stand and rubbed his bleeding arm up and down the length of the strings, coating them in red. Then he began to play, first caressing the bloody instrument, then pounding it ferociously. Finally he smashed the guitar into the drum set – the toms, the snare, bass drum, cymbals - until he had destroyed the entire kit. All the while, he screamed the refrain:

> *My blood is what you what you need,*
> *Cut me now and watch me bleed.*
> *My blood is what you what you need,*
> *Cut me now and watch me bleed.*

Raging like a lunatic, Gravel next tore into the monitors and other sound equipment, with blood splattering left and right, sparks flying, chunks of wood and metal hurtling through the air. Fear took hold of the crowd and they scattered quickly as though they'd come face to face with a demon.

They had.

Finally, I silenced my guitar. The moment I did, Gravel stopped abruptly as if I'd freed him from a trance. He turned toward me and said, "Let's get the hell out of here, Trotter! Now!"

Bobby was speechless, his face white with fear. Gravel pulled huge wads of cash – many thousands of dollars – from his pocket and tossed them toward the stunned bar owner. I grabbed Addie's hand and we ran like the devil back to Gravel's truck and disappeared into the night.

36

There were sirens in the distance – no doubt, headed for The Firehouse – as we rolled up Route 83 toward the Mustang Motel.

Gravel said, "Feels good to be the cause of sirens two days in a row."

"Two days in a row?" Addie asked. "What did you do yesterday?"

"Check your phone and you might see it under breaking news," Gravel said. "Somebody's bound to have figured it out by now."

Addie thumbed her way through several screens and shouted, "Oh, my god, you stabbed a guy?"

"Self-defense," Gravel said.

"You see, that's what I'm talking about," I said. "You stab a guy and don't even tell us about it. That's an important piece of information. What the hell's going on with you anyway?"

"He didn't die," Gravel said.

A momentary silence hit us like a bug on the windshield as a Peterbilt hauling chickens roared by. We pulled into the motel lot, hid the truck in a gully around back, and went inside the room. While Gravel made phone calls, Addie read the news story to me about the fight at the bar in San Angelo, and how the man had attacked Gravel. Then we turned on the television to

CNN, where the anchor, Carol Storm, was giving the latest reports.

"A few hours ago, we reported that a man calling himself Henry Lamartiniere nearly stabbed a man to death in a bar fight. As we revealed then, Henry Lamartiniere is the birth name of music superstar, Gravel Gold, who has been missing for several months. Mr. Gold was allegedly in disguise at the time of the near-fatal encounter, and those following the case closely believe that Mr. Gold has likely been hiding out somewhere in west Texas since his disappearance. Now we have breaking news from Abilene, Texas, and we go to our reporter on the scene. Tom, what can you tell us?"

"Carol, there's been another shocking event in the ongoing saga of Gravel Gold. I'm standing just outside a popular nightclub in Abilene called The Firehouse. According to numerous eye witnesses, Gravel Gold entered the club just a short time ago, jumped up on stage, and gave an impromptu performance."

"Tom, was Mr. Gold alone?" the anchor interjected. "Or did he have other musicians or an entourage with him?"

"Carol, Gravel Gold was apparently accompanied by a young woman – believed to be Addie Dinapolis – and at least one other musician, Trotter Benz, Gravel's longtime guitarist. Many of those who were inside the building at the time said that, after performing for about twenty minutes, Gravel Gold suddenly went berserk and began cutting himself with a hunting knife and smashing everything on stage."

"Was anyone injured?"

"Carol, as you can see behind me, police and emergency vehicles are on the scene, and this is a situation in flux. But so far, we do know that there were at least four minor injuries reported as a result of the ensuing melee. Now, let me bring in a couple of eye

179

witnesses here. Sir, can you describe what you saw tonight?"

The man from the crowd said, "It was totally off the hook, man. Gravel and Trotter were rockin' the house, but then Gravel went nuts, man. I mean crazy like he'd lost his mind. He cut himself up with a big knife and screamed about being the Cajun Voodoo Man. Then he started throwing and smashing equipment, and stuff was blowin' up."

A second eyewitness leaned close to the reporter's microphone and added, "Yeah, glass and metal were flying all over the place. Some of the equipment caught on fire somehow, and people started running just to get out of there. It was totes insane."

"Carol," Tom, the reporter, said. "I also spoke with the owner of the club, Mr. Bobby Benson. Mr. Benson declined to appear on camera at this time, but he did tell me that this was an innocent situation that simply got a little out of hand. He says it was all part of the show, but that Gravel Gold got a little carried away. And he reports that Mr. Gold gave him more than $30,000 to cover any damages resulting from tonight's performance."

"Good ol' Bobby," Gravel said as he abruptly turned off the television.

Addie was giddy. "They said my name on national TV! How cool is that?"

I hugged her and said, "Yeah, you're gonna be famous! Pretty soon you'll dump me because you'll be too snotty to be seen with me."

"That's right, I can't go slumming," Addie said as she did a little dance in the center of the room. "You better keep up with me or I'll drop your ass."

Gravel interrupted our banter. "Grab your stuff. This thing is blowin' up faster than I expected. The spirit says we got to get out of here now."

The spirit says?

"Where are we going?" Addie said.

"We're meetin' Benji and Charles a little ways up the road. Trotter, we're takin' your car cuz somebody probably saw my truck."

"Who the hell is Charles?" I asked, for the second time that evening.

"You'll find out soon enough. Now, come on, Trotter, you're drivin'."

We went farther north on Route 83 beneath a pitch black sky dotted by a million starry eyes. We passed a tiny hamlet called Hamlin and another one called Aspermont. There was almost no other traffic on the old two-lane road, and we rode for an hour in mostly silence.

It was two o'clock in the morning when Gravel said, "Okay, slow down. We should be gettin' close."

"To what?" I asked.

"Look for a dirt road that turns off to the right."

I slowed down and we peered into the darkness.

"There it is," Gravel said. "Turn there and follow it out a ways."

I turned onto the bumpy, dirt trail that was more like a cow path. After half a mile, the road circled behind a stand of short trees and a large cluster of boulders.

"What do we do now?" Addie asked.

"We wait," Gravel said.

I kept quiet; I was tired of asking questions. I figured Gravel would spill the beans when he was finished playing International Man of Mystery. Besides, the whole thing was becoming a bit too absurd for me.

I reached under the seat and pulled out a half-full bottle of vodka. I took a big swig and offered some to Gravel.

"No, I'm good," Gravel said, sounding as though he was a million miles away.

"I've never *ever* seen you refuse a drink before," I said. Then half-joking, I added, "What happened? You find God or something?"

Gravel looked at me very seriously and said, "You can't find what you never lost."

I glanced in the rear view mirror at Addie. She looked just as puzzled as me. "Well, I'll take some," she said.

At three o'clock in the morning, the sound of a helicopter roused us from our drowsiness.

"That's Benji and Charles," Gravel said, as they landed nearby and got out of the chopper.

"Everything good?" Gravel shouted.

"Yes, sir," Benjamin answered. "I brought everything we'll need for tomorrow. Checked it four times to be certain."

"Lord, is he anal," Charles said with a laugh. "In more ways than one."

I extended my hand. "You must be Charles; I'm Trotter."

"Yes, sir, I recognize you from music videos," Charles said. "And also from the news since the three of you made such a stir last night. My Twitter timeline is blowing up with it."

"Yeah, yeah, enough about last night," Gravel said. "Let's focus on today. Benji, give everybody a copy of the map of the town."

Addie looked at hers and asked, "Paducah? That's in Kentucky, right?"

Benjamin said, "There are two towns named Paducah in the United States – one in Kentucky, one in Texas. The one in Texas is barely 1.5 square miles in size and has a population of about one thousand."

Gravel raised his arms toward black heaven and proclaimed, "And tomorrow at high noon, the eyes of the whole world are gonna be zeroed in on that one little dot on the Lone Star map – Paducah, Texas."

37

The tiny town was deathly still and quiet just before dawn as the black sky began to soften in the east. Addie and I were parked directly behind the historic Cottle Hotel, positioned exactly where Gravel instructed us to be, waiting.

"Did you notice that Gravel hasn't had a single drop of alcohol since we met back up with him?" I asked.

"Yeah, very weird," Addie said. "Never seen him so sober."

"And it's like he's talking in riddles or something, you know, trying to be mysterious. He almost seems like he's lost his mind or found God or something."

"I liked the old Gravel way better," Addie observed. "With him, you knew exactly what you were getting."

"True, and now, who knows what's going on? I mean, what are we doing sitting here in Paducah, Texas, behind this abandoned building?"

Neither of us knew the answer, yet, so we sat for a while in silence as Addie worked her phone, and I watched the sky morph from black to gray to a beautiful blend of pastels.

"Hey, hey, here's something," Addie said suddenly. "Story just broke on Twitter. It says Gravel Gold's going to hold a news conference today at noon, central time, in Paducah, Texas."

I furrowed my brow at her. "Here? A news conference *here*? Doesn't make any sense."

"Yeah, why not New York or Los Angeles or even Nashville? He could do it anywhere in the world."

I thought about it for a minute and said, "You know, I guess it does make perfect 'Gravel Gold sense.' I mean, what's more absurd than holding a big press conference somewhere in the middle of nowhere? That sounds like something he'd do just to piss people off."

"Wow, this is crazy!" Addie continued, "They're saying that every major news agency is rushing here to be on the scene for the event."

"Oh, boy," I said. "This could get interesting."

■ ■ ■ ■ ■

By 8:30 am, the locals appeared to be getting the news that something big was about to happen in their small town. Traffic picked up and residents began coming out on their porches and gathering in small clusters of five or ten along the sidewalks, talking excitedly, their curiosity running rampant.

A half hour later, a news helicopter buzzed overhead and landed in a nearby clearing, followed by a second and a third. Soon other reporters and their crews began arriving in large white vans, brightly emblazoned with their stations' call letters and network affiliation. Traffic thickened to a standstill on the small town streets, and in the span of 90 minutes, the crowd grew from dozens to hundreds to thousands. People were now arriving from everywhere within a 300 mile radius – which included the cities of Dallas and Oklahoma City – having jumped in their cars and headed for Paducah as soon as Benjamin issued the first online press release at dawn.

"This is like, totes, insane," Addie said, as we sat hunched down in our seats, watching the spectacle unfold

184

from our inconspicuous and somewhat secluded vantage point.

At exactly 11:00 a.m. my cell phone rang. It was Gravel. "Alright, Trots, it's time. You and Addie get that stuff up on the roof."

We did our best to appear casual as we each took one of the fifty-pound bags from the car, and went to the boarded-up back door of the Cottle Hotel. No one noticed us; there was simply too much else going on to attract attention. Only a dozen or so law enforcement officers had arrived on the scene so far, and they were fully engaged, attempting to maintain control of the large crowds on the main and side streets.

The Cottle Hotel was an historic, three-story building originally built in 1929, but it had been in complete disrepair for many decades. All of the doors and windows on the ground floor were boarded up, and many of the windows on the second and third floors had been broken, no doubt by rock-throwing vandals or rogue Texas twisters.

One of the rear entries to the building provided easy access for us since several of the wooden slats had been loosened and damaged over the years. Once inside, we made our way to the top floor, pushed open an access panel, and put the bags on the roof. After we brought the rest of the bags up as well, we took a few moments to rest.

The sun was warm on our faces as we sat on the roof together, holding hands, and looking for shapes in the clouds. Secluded on top of the building, we could hear the crowd of thousands murmuring and milling around on the ground below, but we couldn't we see them. For those few minutes, it felt as though we'd fallen into some sort of surrealistic dream. We smiled at each other, amused by the on-going absurdity of life with Gravel Gold, and then we kissed. In that moment, I realized why

I loved this young woman named Addie Dinapolis. She was sweet, fun to be with, and not afraid of anything. And though she sometimes displayed girlish immaturity, she always seemed to find a way to roll with whatever life handed her, and to have a good time with it.

"You're pretty amazing," I whispered.

Addie gave me that cute, crooked grin and giggled, "I know." Then she kissed me good.

At 11:45 a.m. the sound of helicopter blades cut through the sky. Most of the people on the ground assumed it was another news team, but I knew better. Charles circled the chopper above the Cottle Hotel and then came in closer, dropping slowly but steadily downward. After touching down on the rooftop, Gravel, Benjamin and Charles jumped out carrying equipment.

"Give us a hand, Trotter," Gravel shouted. "Let's get this set up."

In twenty minutes we had a public address sound system – including speakers, stands, cables, sound board, microphones, laptop and generator – completely connected and ready to operate. We moved the entire arrangement over to the edge of the roof above the main street, and in so doing, got the attention of everyone on the ground. When they spotted Gravel Gold, the steady buzz of the crowd became a rumble of anticipation.

For a few moments, the five of us – Gravel, Benjamin, Charles, Addie and I - gathered in the center of the roof, out of the crowd's line of sight.

"This is it," Gravel said with a bit of solemnity. "This is what it all comes down to."

"And what exactly is that?" I asked. "Are you going to announce your new record? Are you retiring? Announcing your candidacy for President? Moving to Tibet to become a monk? I mean, what the heck is it?"

Gravel gave me a quirky smile and said, "Trotter, what's the best thing about a fireworks show?"

186

I shook my head in frustration. "What does that have to do with anything?"

Charles interjected, "The grand finale."

Gravel nodded approvingly and pointed at him, "Ah, there ya go. Sir Charles. It's all about the big boom at the end. It's gotta be one they'll never forget. Always leave 'em wantin' more."

With that, Gravel turned and walked toward the microphone on the corner of the roof. As he stepped to the edge where the crowd could see him, they exploded with fresh enthusiasm.

Addie wrapped her arm tightly in mine and said, "You think he's gonna do something crazy?"

"Of course," I said.

38

Nearly every major news and entertainment network in the world was in attendance, their cameras trained on Gravel's every word and movement as he stepped out onto the ledge, microphone in hand, to speak to the crowd three stories below. "Ladies and gentlemen, fans and friends, thank you so much for bein' here today."

His voice boomed out of the four powerful speakers, echoed down the streets of Paducah, and brought a massive cheer from his worshipping throng.

"This is an important day in my life, more important than you know; and I'm glad you're all here to share it with me. Ya know, we can do great things in this world when we all pull together, and I truly believe that. Who's with me? Are ya with me?! Come on, let me hear ya!" He pumped his fist in the air repeatedly.

The crowd roared like thunder, so loudly it seemed as if the old hotel was quaking beneath us.

Over the noise, Addie yelled in my ear, "What's he even talking about?"

"Oh, my god," I said. "Maybe I was right...he sounds like he's campaigning for a political office!"

"You think that could be what his big announcement is about?"

"I don't know but it wouldn't surprise me."

Gravel motioned to the crowd to quiet them, and continued, "All the things I've been through in the past year have really changed me, and I stand before you today a new man. I'm makin' this public statement here and now so that all the world will know the truth. Today is my day to come clean, to make things right, and to start over. In America, we believe in second chances, ain't that right?!"

The roar of the crowd escalated to a fever pitch and they began to chant: *Gravel Gold, Gravel Gold, Gravel Gold.*

After a minute, he quieted them again, took some papers from a folder and said, "These here are copies of my divorce papers. I signed 'em a little while back and they've been properly filed. To Gigi, my ex-wife, wherever you are today, I wanna publicly apologize to you. I'm real sorry I hurt ya. And I want ya to know that ya now officially have the divorce that ya wanted and deserved."

Rather than cheering the divorce or Gravel's indiscretions, the crowd murmured with a somewhat solemn tone.

Gravel continued, "I also apologize to the head of my former record label, Jimmy Bolen, and to my former manager, Cotton Black. I said and did some things that I regret, and I hope and pray that they might find forgiveness in their hearts, and that we might someday work together again in the music world."

I leaned over toward Benjamin and said, "Wow, this is amazing. I've never heard Gravel talk like this before. He's definitely saying *all* the right things."

Benjamin gave me an odd, sideways glance and a monotone sort of reply, "Yes, he certainly is, isn't he?"

"Speaking of music," Gravel said. "I have a brand new recording, an album of twelve new songs. I believe with all my heart that this is the best record I've ever made, the best songs of my life. Any of you folks want to hear a little bit of it?"

The people on the streets below went nuts.

Gravel reached over and pushed a button on the soundboard and a short clip from one of his new songs began to play. The music was rhythmic, beautiful and entrancing; and the crowd of thousands swayed as one. Then the glorious lyrics rang out:

I'm sifting through the pieces of my life,
Scattered about on the floor,
Somebody hand me a knife,
Don't think I can take much more.

Even the best of intentions,
Sometimes just ain't enough,
When ya lose your sense of direction,
It's hard to find your way back to love.

I have moved my last mountain,
Don't have to prove a damn thing,
I have drunk deep from the fountain,
Where the angels dip their wings.

I'm nearer the end now than it seems,
Sketching my life as I ramble,
Sometimes these nightmares and dreams,
Are more than I can handle.

My back is weary from my heavy load,
Life is hard on the gravel road,
Yeah, my back is weary from my heavy load
Life is hard on the gravel road.

The song swept over me, breaking me as the Pacific breaks on black rock, swirling and churning at the mouth of the Columbia River. Just like everyone else who was there that day, I marveled at the glory of Gravel's creation. There was no denying the audible facts, the inescapable evidence - his record was a masterpiece of obliterating beauty and unadulterated majesty. I stood there on that rooftop, in the midst of that surreal scene, and I wept.

As the crowd once again chanted his name, Gravel Gold stood there on the ledge for several minutes, waving to them, and repeating, "Thank you all for comin' today. Thank you for believin' in me all these years. I love ya, I truly do. To all my fans all over the world, I love each and every one of ya. May the good Lord bless you all."

Gravel turned and came quickly toward us. There were tears in his eyes. "Charles, start that thing up," he shouted. "We're gonna do some victory laps for the people!"

Charles jumped in the chopper and quickly had it ready to take off.

"Trotter, you're with me," Gravel said. "Benji, you stay here with Addie and handle anything that comes up. I figure I broke a bunch of codes and ordinances. Police will probably wanna talk to somebody about unlawful assembly without a permit, public endangerment, creatin' a public disturbance or whatever."

"Alright, Mr. Gold," Benjamin said. "I will take care of things on the ground."

Gravel and I boarded the helicopter and Charles guided us up and away from the Cottle House.

"Take us up a few thousand feet or so," Gravel shouted. "Then circle around the town a couple times to build the anticipation, before bringin' us back in real low so I can wave to the folks."

"Yes, sir," Charles said.

From high up, Paducah looked just like so many other tiny Texas towns; a small cluster of perfect squares

191

framed by roads at right angles, sitting alone in the middle of a vast expanse of scrub brush.

Gravel put his arm around my shoulders, leaned in close and said, "My new record's gonna be the biggest seller of all time."

I nodded vigorously, "I know, I know it is."

"And best of all, after the way I've arranged things, Gigi, Bolen and Cotton won't see one damn cent from it. No sir, not the first penny. And if anything was to ever happen to me, I've set things up so that all my money goes to my aunt Anna Marie, Benji, you, and the Native Americans."

Native Americans?

Gravel had given me far too much information in only a few seconds, and it was difficult to process all at once, especially in such a fast-moving, high-pressure situation. I had no idea how to respond, so I simply kept quiet.

Gravel pointed and said, "See all them people down there, Trotter? They cheer for me and chant my name, but they don't know me at all, and they don't really love me. They love what I represent to 'em, what I give 'em. It's the music that speaks to somethin' deep in their hearts, somethin' they can't even understand. Hell, I don't understand it either. Nobody can."

I looked down at the town as we circled it. A tiny hamlet far out in the middle of nowhere had increased its population by at least five thousand in just a couple of hours, and all because one man said, *Come.*

"Remember what I said about a fireworks show?"

"Yeah, the grand finale is what matters most," I answered.

Gravel recited a list of names, "Kurt Cobain, Ernest Hemingway, James Dean, Chris Farley, Elvis Presley, Marilyn Monroe, John Lennon…I could go on and on. What do they all have in common, Trotter?"

"Uh, well," I said, thinking about it for a moment. "Those are stars that committed suicide or died in some tragic way."

"Exactly. They all left this world in a shocking way, with a bang and not with a whimper. And that's what people remember the most, the bang. It's the icin' on the cake."

"Okay, so what's your point?"

Before Gravel answered my question, Charles said, "Mr. Gold, you ready to take those victory laps now?"

"Yeah, it's time," Gravel said. "Take us down to where they can get a good look at me. Maybe a hundred or even just fifty feet or so off the ground...I'll trust your judgment on the altitude, but get us as low as you possibly can."

We looped down over the Cottle Hotel and I waved to Addie who was jumping up and down excitedly on the roof. Then we flew slowly along the main street and the astounding roar of the crowd rose up to meet us in midair, almost drowning out the noise of the helicopter. Gravel leaned out the open door of the chopper, waving and shouting to his fans all the way.

"Give us a couple more passes, Charles!" Gravel shouted, caught up in the rush of it all.

So we went to the west edge of town, turned and came at them from the opposite direction. While holding onto the hand grip, Gravel stepped out onto the landing skid like some kind of daredevil stunt man.

"Gravel, are you crazy?" I screamed. "Get back in here!"

"Relax, Trotter. I know what I'm doin'," Gravel shouted. "I wanna show my fans how much I love 'em."

We made a long, swooping turn up and around before coming back in to make one last pass over the crowd and the old hotel. As we did, Gravel's feet suddenly slipped off the skid, and everyone on the ground gasped and

193

screamed. For a few moments, Gravel hung there by one hand, dangling, his legs flailing and searching instinctively for something, anything solid to latch onto. Charles fought to steady the helicopter as the sudden shift of Gravel's 250 pound frame caused the craft to tip and wobble.

I lunged toward Gravel, desperately trying to grab hold of him without falling out of the chopper myself, but I couldn't reach him.

"Down, down, down!" I screamed at Charles. "Take us down!"

But it all happened so quickly, like the blink of an eye or a shooting star across the sky.

Gravel's grip loosened and he began to slip. Smiling deviously, he shouted to me over the roar of the chopper blades, "I told ya, Trotter! Mark my words: *biggest selling record of all time!*"

And then, with the whole world watching, on a bright, sunny afternoon, Gravel Gold plummeted two hundred feet onto the roof of the historic Cottle Hotel in Paducah, Texas, where he was impaled right through the heart on his very own microphone stand. Blood exploded from his body like a red rain of redemption, and left a fine, crimson mist hanging in the air over his worshippers.

Bang.